EV
IE

# VIOLET
# SLAYS

USA TODAY BESTSELLING AUTHOR

# LEXI C. FOSS

*Violet Slays*

Editing by: Outthink Editing, LLC

Proofreading by: Katie Schmahl, Jean Bachen & Julie Robertson

Cover Design: Francesca Michelon with Merry-Book-Round Covers

Published by: Ninja Newt Publishing, LLC

Digital ISBN: 978-1-954183-38-4

Print ISBN: 978-1-954183-39-1

❀ Created with Vellum

# VIOLET SLAYS

Eliminate Vampiric Influences Everywhere.
That's my life.
My job.
My entire world.

I fell victim to a vampire once. He used me to commit the ultimate crime of betrayal. A consequence I've lived with for over a century thanks to the immortality amulet around my neck.

Now I slay every bloodsucker in sight.
Which is why they call me the "demon of the night."

My E.V.I.E. boss has a new assignment for me—some errant vamp causing issues in New York City. No problem. I'll handle this pest like I have the countless leeches before him.

Only this is no ordinary vampire.
It's Cassius.
My former lover.
My betrayer.
The royal vampire who seduced me into a forbidden affair that nearly ended my life.

Seeing him again is a blow to the chest, one I intend to return with a stake through his dead heart.
Because I don't do second chances, a fact Cassius is about to learn the hard way.

*Stake up, friends. It's going to be a bloody ride.*

# VIØLET

## CHAPTER ONE

SILVER EYES.

Glistening.

Deadly.

Seductive.

I moaned, fighting the need coursing through me at that familiar look—the one that demanded my submission. Craved my blood. Destroyed my resolve.

This was so wrong. Forbidden. A lethal dance.

"Beg," he demanded, his deep voice undoing the last of my willpower.

My knees hit the carpet, my lips parting on a foreign plea for him to take me. Complete me. Make me *his*.

Full lips curled at the sides, a hint of menace darkening his handsome features. "I like you in this position, little slayer," he mused, his fingers reaching out to lightly comb through my hair. "Compliant and mine."

My instincts dared me to fight, to prove him wrong, but my heart held me captive. I wanted this. He wanted this. It didn't matter what anyone else thought. The rules be damned. *This* was my soul's purpose. *He* was my lifeline.

That sinister look deepened, his long white hair seemed to unfurl beneath a mysterious wind as he leaned down to stare me directly in the eyes.

1

Anger blazed from the depths of his silvery gaze, swirling deep within, threatening to flay me alive. "I'm coming for you, sweet slayer," he vowed.

I frowned, not understanding. Then he released me and took a step back, his body vanishing into a dusky cloud.

And I opened my eyes to reveal a new room.

*My* room.

In Chicago.

Not in Saint Petersburg.

Not in my former realm.

Not in the life I left behind.

But my current reality. Where vampires couldn't walk in the daylight and died by stakes.

No fire here.

No meaningless death.

No Romanov slayers.

Just those involved with Eliminate Vampiric Influences Everywhere, or E.V.I.E., as we usually referred to it.

"Shit." I grasped the amulet hanging from my neck, my chest heaving from the too-real dream.

*I'm coming for you, sweet slayer.*

How many times had he promised me that? I'd always taken that phrase as a heated flirtation. Until the true meaning of his threat became a reality that ended in bloodshed.

Oh, he came for me all right.

And the entire Romanov slayer line as well.

Swallowing, I glanced sideways at my clock. It was three in the afternoon. A perfectly safe time to sleep, but I wouldn't be catching any more *z*'s after that dream.

Rubbing a hand over my face, I sat up. My bare legs were covered in sweat, my inner thighs were too warm, and my nipples were hard. All because of *Cassius.*

Just thinking his name sent a shiver down my spine.

His too-pretty face flashed behind my eyes, his lips curling into his trademark smirk. He was hot and he knew it. A prince with a savage streak and a penchant for domination. I'd never knelt for another male. Not before him or after him. And I never would after everything he'd done to me.

Shaking my head, I rolled out of bed and prepared for my early evening run several hours ahead of schedule. I needed to pound the cement for at least thirty minutes, and then maybe head to the gym for a round with the punching bag. If only I had a photo of Cassius to mount on it; I'd beat him to a bloody pulp.

My skin prickled with the memories of the last time I saw him. Heat wrapped around me, suffocating my throat, drawing me back into a smoke-infused room littered with flames.

*Residual screams abrade my eardrums.*
*I can't breathe.*
*I'm going to die here.*
*In this place.*
*Because of him.*
*He's the only one who knows—*

My wrist buzzed, drawing me out of the darkness and back into the light. Over a century in this realm and I still hadn't forgotten that night—the one that altered my entire world. Literally.

I ignored the second message coming in across my watch and went straight for the coffee maker. Technology had vastly improved over my lifetime, yielding amazing inventions such as the instant pot before me.

*Ah, sweet, sweet addiction.* I smiled. *Pour for me, baby.*

Pressing a few buttons caused the device to spring to life, and the sensual aroma of bliss began to fill the air.

My bestie, Rowan, hated coffee—a fact that nearly ended our friendship, because seriously, who could hate heavenly caffeine? But I forgave her. Sort of like how I forgave her for somehow using her witch magic to portal three of us into the E.V.I.E. world. She'd been trying to save our lives, and had succeeded, so there was that tidbit.

Of course, the experience had turned my hair a startling purple shade. Rowan's had turned a silvery lavender, but the hair of the other slayer who'd traveled here with us had remained green. *Bright* green. Hence her original name —Emerald.

I'd changed my name to Violet to match for fun.

And because my given name in Russian brought back too many memories.

I drummed my fingers across the granite counter, watching as my mug began to change colors. It'd been a gift from Rowan. The ceramic exterior was black when cold and slowly melted into an image when warmth touched it.

*Unicorn Badass II* displayed in white lettering with a purple-haired unicorn beneath, making me smile.

"Damn straight." I picked up the mug as soon as it finished, added a splash of creamer to cool it, and took a hearty sip. It burned so good going down.

Only when I was halfway done did I finally venture back to my bedroom to look at the messages on my phone. They were all from Jude—the head of E.V.I.E.

*I need you in New York City.*

*Like, now.*

*Get up.*

I snorted and set my mug down on the nightstand to shoot him back a message. *You sure know how to seduce a girl, J.* I tossed my phone onto the unmade bed, then headed to the en-suite bathroom to take a shower since clearly a run wasn't on the agenda now, thanks to work.

Not that I minded.

It'd been a few weeks since I'd given my stake a workout.

Stripping down to just my amulet, I stepped beneath the warm spray of my double-headed shower and allowed the water to wash away the memories of my dream.

Or was it a nightmare?

I couldn't tell the difference.

My body apparently thought it was a fantasy. My stomach still coiled with a need only Cassius could awaken, even after all this time, and the memories of him remained solidly in my head. For all I knew, the bastard was dead.

I grunted. *Right.*

Prince Cassius was probably lording over the other realm, aiding his king, Dimitri, in thaeir quest to destroy the human race. All because I'd given Cassius the codes.

My palm hit the stone wall, a growl leaving my mouth.

Rowan would tell me to stop fretting. No, she'd berate me for not letting this go after a century. But it wasn't her fault that an entire line of slayers fell all because of a forbidden affair. Instead, she'd saved me when I hadn't deserved to be saved.

Groaning, my elbow bent, and I pressed my forehead to the stone and began to count.

Ten seconds.

That was all I would allow myself to feel today.

Just ten seconds of sorrow and pain.

Then I'd wake the fuck up and get to work. Because there were vampires to kill. And oh, how I loved to slay them.

As soon as I hit one in my head, I straightened my spine and shoved the memories away.

Twenty minutes later, I was dressed in a pair of jeans, boots, and a sweater. Fall in New York City ranged in temperatures, as did Chicago. I added stakes to the wardrobe, all obscured from human view, and slipped a knife into a hidden compartment along the side of my pants before adding my phone to the back pocket. Purple hair up in a ponytail, face void of makeup, I was ready to go.

Minus one thing.

Luci.

She lounged on my sofa—her chosen bed—and gave me a lazy yawn as I entered. "I know you heard me in the kitchen," I told her. "It's right over there." Like ten feet away from the medium-sized living room. My condo was a bit on the small side with just the one bedroom, one and a half baths, a kitchen, and a living room, but it worked for the two of us.

She yawned again, adding in a lick of her chops at the end to drive her point home. *It's early.*

"Yeah, I know," I said.

Her long black lashes began to close, hiding her pretty brown eyes.

"Does that mean you want to stay here instead of munching on some vampires?" I asked her.

One eye opened.

"We have to use the portal," I added. Because no way would I ever try to fly with my baby. She had a penchant for setting things on fire. Hence the burn marks on my supposedly flame-retardant couch.

Turns out, they don't make upholstery suitable for hellhounds. Who knew?

Luci slowly slid off the couch, her black fur sleek and freshly brushed from last night.

Because yeah, I doted on her wolf form. Not that I didn't appreciate her hellhound glory, but it was just harder to pet her when her pores oozed fire.

She gave a long stretch of her back legs, reminding me of a German Shepherd, then loosened up her front similarly before shaking out her coat.

Her intelligent coffee-brown irises met mine, the

knowledge in them setting her apart from the wolf form. She couldn't speak, but she understood me perfectly. Making commands unnecessary.

"Ready?" I asked.

She gave another shake, which was her equivalent of an affirmation.

"Try to stay in wolf form," I said, walking over to the basket in the small foyer by my front door. "Last time you went hellhound, you scared a few kids."

She huffed in reply.

"Yeah, I know, he was a little prick." The kid had been bullying another, and Luci wasn't a fan of that behavior.

Her grunt sounded like an agreement.

I grabbed her collar and bent down to put the red nylon around her thick neck. She didn't really need it, but humans preferred I walked her on a leash, so we put on a show to keep the mortals happy.

Most humans weren't aware of the supernatural. Only the unlucky few knew the truth. Slayers included.

"All right," I said, securing the leash with one hand.

I clutched the amulet hanging between my breasts with my opposite palm and flicked my thumb over the oval-shaped tanzanite at the center, opening a portal. It flared to life naturally, the magic ingrained in the enchanted stone.

Learning how to navigate the portal network had been a decade-long process, one Rowan had helped me with. Jude didn't know our amulets allowed us to travel this way, but he knew they were enchanted, particularly as they made us immortal.

Whenever I removed it, I aged normally—one day at a time—but I rarely took off the amulet. I didn't want to risk losing it. I also enjoyed being in my early twenties.

The fur along Luci's back edged upward in alert as soon as we stepped through the portal, her guarding instincts taking over. Some of the paths went through the underworld, which was how I'd found my little hellhound.

She'd been curled into a fiery little ball with pointy ears, shivering in a corner. When a vampire attacked me in front of her—he'd followed me through my portal—she'd taken off his leg as a snack. It'd been love at first sight between us after that.

We wandered along the dark corridor framed by oozing liquids that were not meant to be touched. I sometimes wondered if this was really the underworld or just a pathway through space and time. Luci's existence made me think it was the former, but I rarely found life here. It was possible someone had led her here and then left her to fend for herself.

I frowned at the notion, as I did every time I considered it.

"You know I'll kill anyone who touches you, right?" I said to her now as we walked.

She snorted, then glanced up at me with murder in her gaze. *Likewise*, she seemed to be saying.

"We make a good team."

She grunted in agreement, then shook out her coat.

"Yeah, I'm not a fan of it down here either." The black-coated walls moved ominously, making it very dark. But little specks of light from above lit the way like stars in the night. Or maybe those were glowworms. Who the hell knew? I never stuck around long enough to find out.

A few minutes later, I took a left, then a right, and then another left and found myself on the precipice of the New York City portal. While I could see through the shimmering space, no one else could see me—something Rowan and I had tested ample times.

I glanced through the glittering curtain before me, watching the space for any signs of life.

I usually created my own entry within the existing one, which allowed me to rejoin the realm as though I were walking fresh out of the main portal. But I had to make sure the coast was clear first.

If anyone touched me along the way, it could complicate things. And as Jude had the place wired with security, I couldn't risk him catching me creating my own entrance, so I had to time it right.

It wasn't that we didn't trust Jude; we just preferred to keep our pasts to ourselves. And we were protecting Emerald, too.

If he knew what she was, he'd try to recruit her, and our friend had made it clear she wanted nothing to do with the underworld life. She'd run off to open up a tattoo parlor in Columbus, Ohio, and seemed to be doing pretty well for herself.

"Okay, Luci," I said, stepping into the space right before the portal opening. "Let's go."

# CASSIUS

## CHAPTER TWO

*KSENIYA.*

She looked different with sleek purple waves instead of soft blonde strands and startling violet eyes rather than soft blue ones. But the rest of her resembled my pet slayer—petite frame, toned limbs, pert breasts, and a supple waist. My mouth watered just looking at her, making me rethink my plans for later.

Over a century of hatred boiled inside me, underlined in a sea of blossoming lust just at the sight of my sweet slayer.

I wanted to strangle her.

Fuck her.

Make her bleed.

Then lick her to completion before driving a stake between her ribs. What a fitting end that would be.

I trailed behind her as she walked through the streets of Manhattan without a care in the world. The black dog at her side glanced at me more than once, her eyes much too intelligent for a canine. But she didn't alert her owner to my presence, her tongue hanging out of her mouth in a wolflike grin that made her almost appear kind.

*Good girl,* I thought at the creature before focusing on Kseniya's fine ass. She wore a pair of snug jeans that drew more than a few male glances her way as she moved. She just had one of those bodies that men wanted to caress.

I could still remember the first time I saw her sparring with one of her fellow slayers in one of Catherine Palace's many courtyards.

She'd been a sight to behold, and when she'd finished, I strolled by and asked if she wanted a more worthy opponent. Her gorgeous blue eyes had flared wide, her lips parting at the sight of a vampire so close to her sacred slayer homeland.

We'd fought.

I'd won.

But rather than kill her, I'd pressed my lips to her raging pulse and fled.

We'd engaged in several similar encounters after that, all ending with me disarming her and pinning her to the ground, until one night when she managed to best me with a stake aimed directly for my chest. Only, she hadn't struck me hard enough to kill me. Instead, she'd wavered.

And that was when I'd first kissed her.

My lips tingled with the memory, my body tightening with the urge to do it all over again. That was what this female did to me. One sight of her and my entire plan for revenge faltered.

She'd left me to rot in Grigori's prison for ninety-two very long years. Had Dimitri not found a way to get me out, I'd still be there today.

Because of her.

Because she'd disappeared.

I narrowed my eyes at the back of her purple head. She would pay for what she'd done to me. Visions of her weeping and covered in blood graced the back of my eyes, causing my cock to stir with interest.

I desired her pain.

Craved it.

And would ensure she felt the same anguish I'd experienced in that prison.

Oh, how I'd take pleasure in her tears. My sweet little killer would be an incoherent mess when I finished with her. I couldn't fucking wait.

She continued her path toward E.V.I.E.'s headquarters— this realm's slayer institute. I snorted at the prospect. *What a joke.* They had nothing on the Romanov slayer line back home. Of course, the vampires of this world weren't anything like my brethren.

They couldn't walk in the sun. They hated garlic. They burst into flames from a stake through the heart, then turned to ash. And they had no royalty.

Dimitri would scoff at them all and demand their extermination. Then he'd repopulate the realm with his own brand of vampires. Daywalkers who didn't mind a little garlic in their food and required more than a stake through the heart to die. Oh, it'd slow us down, but we could only be killed by removing our heads. And some of us even required a little fire to completely die.

The slayers of my world were well equipped in the art of staking followed by beheading. It made me wonder how much of those talents Kseniya had maintained in my absence.

I cocked my head to the side, taking in her sensual form once more.

Kseniya crossed the street, heading right toward the entrance of her employer. I stopped to observe, enjoying the view of her hips moving with each step.

Tonight, we'd dance.

She just didn't know it yet.

*See you soon, little slayer,* I thought at her, my lips curling at the sides. *You'll look so pretty on your knees.*

Her dog glanced back at me as though she could hear

me, her wolfy grin closing. I gave her a little wave, then turned away to prepare for my date with Kseniya.

It'd taken me nearly three months to prepare and several years before that to find her. Had it not been for Dimitri's connection to the witch community, I might never have learned the importance of those slayer amulets. *That* was how my Kseniya had slipped between my fingers. Her vampire-witch friend, Rowan, had engaged the spell to transport her to this alternate reality, and they'd hidden here ever since.

When I'd discovered how easy it was to transfer back and forth, my ire had reached a high point.

Kseniya could have come back to me at any time and chose not to.

Because she'd left me to die in that cell.

A cell she could have infiltrated and pulled me out of yet didn't.

I loathed her.

Yearned for her.

Wanted to wreck her for everything she'd ever done to me. What was left of my soul still desired her, a fact that could only be mitigated by her death.

So maybe I would kill her.

After I played with her.

Tormented her.

Fucked her.

*Destroyed* her.

My devious little slayer.

My love.

My *end*.

I curled my fingers into a fist as I walked, ready for this to be over and excited for it to begin.

Tonight would be the inception of our mutual demise.

And I couldn't wait to watch us burn.

# CHAPTER THREE

LUCI TROTTED ALONG BESIDE ME, her tongue flopping out of her mouth happily. It gave her a less aggressive look and helped her resemble a friendly dog more than a ferocious wolf.

All part of the facade.

When we reached E.V.I.E.'s headquarters—a skyscraper littered with windows—I found Alaric waiting for me. I arched a brow at the sexy slayer in the pristine marble lobby. "Looking for a sparring partner?" I asked him.

"You wish," he replied, turning to walk with me through security. His broad shoulders were twice the width of mine and all muscle.

The dude spent a lot of time working on his physique. It helped with his stamina on a gym mat, marking him as one of the few slayers who could best me in a fight. Which was why I enjoyed our little matches—he provided the competition I craved, something I hadn't experienced since Cassius.

Ignoring the shiver that traversed my spine at the thought of *him*, I continued toward the main security team.

They didn't ask me to disarm. Nor did they ask me to leave Luci outside. Instead, they allowed me to flow through my own line with Alaric a few steps ahead. He didn't say anything more until we were in the elevator heading up to Jude's office.

"How you doin', Luci?" he asked, giving her a dimpled smile.

She bumped her head against his jean-clad thigh in response, asking for a scratch behind the ear.

"Flirt," I murmured, talking to them both.

"Females love me," Alaric replied, his tone as playful as always. Nothing would ever happen between us, but I enjoyed the casual attention, just as I knew he enjoyed mine.

"Any idea what was so urgent that Jude called me in?" The boss man typically let me do my own thing, allowing me to report in to the local area superior of wherever I decided to live.

I'd been with E.V.I.E. for decades, mostly in the European cells, but I'd recently relocated to Chicago. That was when Jude—the head of E.V.I.E.—had requested to meet me for the first time.

He'd sent Casti to fetch me from a portal. The slayer had thought I was a real being from hell, thanks to his physical description. I quickly divested her of that notion, then she'd gone off on some tangent about a pet bat. As my only experience was with Luci, I wasn't of much help to her.

Luci's ears perked up as we reached Jude's floor, her tail beginning to wag in earnest. I removed her leash, knowing what she wanted, and smirked as she bounded out of the elevator, right for Hades.

The male black shepherd was waiting for her in a play bow, and the two began running circles around the executive area outside of Jude's office.

"I guess you don't need to be announced," Alaric drawled.

"Never do," I replied. "And you never answered my question."

"Because I don't have an answer. He told me he wanted to meet with both of us and to wait for you down in the lobby."

I pressed a palm to my heart, feigning a sad look. "And here I thought you just wanted to see me."

"I always want to see you, baby," he tossed back, winking one pretty blue eye at me.

"Stop flirting and get your asses in here," Jude demanded from inside his office.

"It's telling that he thinks that's flirting," Alaric murmured.

"Isn't it?" I agreed, glancing at Luci. She was sprawled out on her back with Hades's jaws wrapped around her throat in a playful bite. They were evenly matched in size, making them ideal playmates. For whatever reason, she seemed to enjoy letting him win.

I left them to their dominance games and followed Alaric into Jude's sprawling office. He sat behind his executive desk, his dark eyes on his computer.

"Nice suit," I told him, plopping down into the chair across from him. Alaric took the other with a smirk, indulging in my sarcasm.

We were always ribbing the boss for his fashion sense. There wasn't anything actually wrong with Jude's attire. The man pulled off the handwoven Italian three-piece suit quite well. Alaric and I just enjoyed trying to rile him up.

Alas, Jude didn't smile or react.

Instead, he pursed his full lips, his focus still on his screen. Whatever held his attention seemed important, which made sense. He wouldn't call me here for a friendly chat.

After a beat, he spun the screen around to show me. "We have a problem."

I studied the image, noting the female's face and clear marks on her neck. It wasn't until I realized the source of the photo that I followed the "problem" he referred to. The dead woman had made media headlines.

"Looks like someone snacked on the wrong heiress," I muttered. It came out sarcastic because that was how I operated, but Jude knew my personality enough to understand I meant that statement as a concern. "What are they claiming as the cause of death?"

The exsanguination was as clear as day, but humans didn't know about vampires, so they always came up with outlandish notions to support the otherwise obvious culprit.

Jude brought up another series of images. "Several other murder files have been pulled in conjunction with Valaria Crimson's death, all believed to be conducted by the same culprit. The media has nicknamed him the Bloodsucker Serial Killer."

"Why am I just now hearing about this?" Alaric asked.

"It wasn't front-page news until Valaria Crimson's death," he replied. "The other victims weren't as famous."

"Meaning no one cared until a beloved heiress lost her life," I translated. "But you've seen the reports of the others." It wasn't a question but a statement. Because I knew this man. He had teams who scoured media for this type of story.

"Of course. And I already have leads for you to investigate." He pushed away from his desk to stand, his height and stance impressive.

The middle-aged male might spend most of his day behind a desk, but he was still in top shape and a force to be reckoned with. I'd challenged him once to a sparring match. He'd proven himself admirable, his old-fashioned techniques still very much relevant.

Our duel had ended in a draw, neither of us able to best the other. And my respect for him had only grown since.

Jude dropped a file in Alaric's lap. "That's the lead for you to explore."

I leaned forward to see the contents inside. "A map?"

"Of nightclubs," Alaric finished. "These are all known vamp havens. What do you want me to do, waltz inside, show them my stake, and demand answers?"

"Those four clubs are the closest to the kill sites. I want to know who is frequenting them. Use tech surveillance to find out." Jude handed Alaric a set of keys. "You know where to go."

The dark-haired slayer grinned. "Spy heaven."

I rolled my eyes. "You and your romantic attachment to technology are starting to concern me, Ric."

I never called him Alaric out loud. Always Ric. It was faster and frequently earned me a scowl. But not today. The pretty boy slayer was too excited by the opportunity to go play with Jude's fancy tech gadgets.

"And for you, I have a tracking mission." Jude handed me a piece of thick card stock with elegant writing on it.

I read through the invitation with a furrowed brow. "You want me to attend a charity ball?" I looked up at him. "Have you lost your goddamn mind?"

"There's a new player in the vampire community. Some ancient calling himself King Kaos. No one has seen his face yet, but he's hosting that fundraiser tonight, and I want to know more about him."

"I'd rather find the serial killer," I deadpanned. "Or put me in the tech suite with Ric. I promise we'll play nice."

"What kind of ancient vampire hosts a fundraiser?" Alaric asked.

"The name Kaos keeps floating around the supernatural community, and I want to know why," he continued as though neither of us had spoken. "I don't know if it's related, but the deaths started shortly after his arrival."

"Send someone else," I pressed. "Gowns are not my thing. Give me a coven to raid instead. I excel in blood, not frivolous conversation."

"It's rumored he's a descendant of the Romanovs," Jude added, meeting my gaze. "Or some royal Russian ancestry. Of course, it's all speculation in the supernatural community, but the point remains—I want to know more about him. And why he's chosen now to make an appearance in my city."

"Romanovs?" Alaric repeated. "Isn't there some sort of cartoon about the missing princess of something?"

"Anastasia," I breathed, very familiar with the story. Only, my world held a different tale than the one told in this reality. And while Jude had never pressed me for details on my background, this case proved he knew a lot more than he'd ever let on before.

I needed to warn Rowan.

"How can you have so much detail about a vampire who has never been photographed?" Alaric asked. "If he's hosting a charity gala, surely someone knows him."

"He's the talk of the town and the newest wealth to move to Upper Manhattan. The rumors of his ties to royalty have only ramped up the intrigue." My boss returned to his seat behind his desk. "Everyone wants to see his face and find out if all the myths are true."

"And you're sure he's a vampire?" Alaric pressed. "Not just some new-money bachelor looking for a society launch?"

Jude shook his head. "Our neutral contacts have confirmed he's some sort of ancient. The vampires are worshipping at his feet, and they don't do that for just anyone."

*Neutral contacts*, I repeated to myself with a mental snort. That translated to bloodsuckers who were willing to provide him with information in exchange for their lives. So long as they remained good little leeches, E.V.I.E. allowed them to continue existing.

However, the moment they stepped out of line, it became open hunting season.

And I *loved* open hunting season.

"What's his name?" I asked. The invitation just mentioned a hosting company—The Amber Foundation.

"Alexander Ivanovich," Jude replied.

*Russian.* I frowned. "Have you found anything else on him or his company?"

"No. Which is why you're going to his fundraiser tonight to see what information you can pick up. Watch and observe only." Jude slid a card across the desk. "You have an appointment in two hours for hair, makeup, and dress selection. I recommend dark red or black."

My eyes narrowed at that slight taunt in his tone. So unlike Jude, the serious former assassin who danced with death more than with people. "I had no idea you were interested in retiring early, boss."

"Be sure to take photos," he added, lacing his fingers before him, his expression giving nothing away. "I'm certain the others would love to see them. We could do a monthly newsletter."

"I love that idea," Alaric agreed. "You could headline it 'Princess Violet Hunts Prince Charming at the Ball.'"

Jude actually wrote it down.

And I wanted to kill them both.

"If this proves to be completely unrelated to the idiot leaving a body trail, I'm going to demand a raise." I stood up and turned toward the door, only to find Luci and Hades cuddling on one of his oversized pet beds just inside. My gaze slowly returned to my boss, a smile forming at the edges of my mouth. "I assume dogs aren't permitted at the fundraiser?"

His dark eyes met mine. "Vi—"

"So you won't mind watching Luci for me tonight, right?"

All signs of amusement vanished. Not that he'd really exuded much emotion before, just a slight twinkle to his dark eyes that had died behind a sea of storm clouds.

"Absolutely not," he snapped. "Her last visit ended in nearly ten thousand dollars' worth of damage."

"Oh, come on. It's not her fault your pretentious penthouse wasn't Luci-proof." Some pet parents dealt with teething problems. Meanwhile, I had a hellhound who occasionally set things on fire. Big deal. We all had our issues.

"No, Violet. I'm not taking her for the night."

I shrugged. "Fine. She can just stay here, and I'll grab her later."

"Violet."

"Jude."

He stared me down in that darkly powerful way of his, but I stared right back. Then casually stepped to the side so he could see Hades and Luci lounging together in the dog bed. The moment his gaze dropped to his precious baby, his features softened.

I waited.

*Five.*

*Four.*

*Three.*

He grumbled something under his breath.

*Two.*

"Fine," he muttered, rubbing a hand down his face. "But if she sets my living room on fire again, you're paying for the damages and emotional compensation."

"Emotional compensation?" I repeated, arching a brow. "Seriously?"

"It was a traumatic experience for Hades last time. He lost one of his favorite toys."

"You mean the stuffed dinosaur I replaced that he loves as much as the original?" I deadpanned.

"It's not the same."

"Uh-huh." I slipped the appointment card into my pocket, then folded my invitation into the other. Walking over to Luci, I pressed a kiss to her head. "Try not to set the couch on fire, okay?"

She gave me a sleepy yawn, then nuzzled back into Hades.

I took that to mean she'd do whatever the hell she wanted, as per her usual.

"See you later, Jude," I said, purposely not mentioning a time to pick up Luci after the charity ball.

He'd probably call to check in around midnight and request a time then. By one, he'd realize my intentions to leave her at his place all night. And by six, I'd probably receive some sort of threat against my life. That would be when I'd make him promise to never give me such a ridiculous assignment ever again.

*A fundraiser to spy on a supposed royal vampire.* I snorted. Even if he had ties to the Romanovs—which I doubted—it would be from this realm, not my own.

Maybe he said all that as a test to see how I would react.

Frowning, I pulled my phone out to send a note to Rowan. She replied by the time I hit the ground floor.

I sent her the location of a local diner near her flat, asking her to meet, and she shot back a thumbs-up.

My lips kicked up, and I started to trek toward the greasy diner I favored. They had an all-day breakfast I loved, and I could use a quick bite before the pampering appointment.

I could go for some coffee, too, since I'd left my barely touched mug on the nightstand back in Chicago.

*Sweet, sweet caffeine. Yes, please.*

Then I'd tell Rowan about the potential Romanov link, as

well as Jude's typical cryptic manner. That man knew more than he let on and played all his cards close to the vest. I'd admire him for it if it didn't irk me so much.

Of course, he probably thought the same about me.

And he'd be right.

# CASSIUS

## CHAPTER FOUR

I WATCHED as Roskana Sokolov sipped her tea, then flinched at the hot liquid scalding her mouth. She had the same purple-colored hair as my Kseniya, only with a slight silvery glimmer to it.

Why had they chosen such odd traits? Was it meant to help them fit in with the current times of this realm?

Roskana used to have red hair, which seemed to pair well against Kseniya's blonde strands. Now they both reminded me of a spring holiday. Far too cheery and bright.

I frowned, sipping my coffee from the shadows. They had no idea I sat so close, too lost in their conversation and togetherness to realize a true predator lurked among them.

The poor little slayers thought they were safe in the early evening sun. The vampires they'd grown accustomed to wouldn't come out for another hour, maybe two. And neither of them was expecting me.

Oh, but my sweet Kseniya would see me soon. What color gown would she wear tonight? Would it be revealing or conservative?

I pictured her in a myriad of outfits, each one bloody and torn as she lay helpless on the ground, whimpering at my feet.

My cock hardened at the prospect.

She would look so pretty in a pool of death. Weeping. Begging me to save her.

Maybe I would, just to play with her a little longer. Turn her into a shadow of her former self, a broken shell with jagged lines and cruel fractures.

Mmm, yes. I liked the sound of that.

I'd been planning this moment for so long that I was almost sad to have it arrive. Because the moment she realized I was here, in her realm, the countdown would begin.

A dangerous dance.

A fucked-up fate.

A perfect end.

I'd survived for this moment alone, the one where I finally made my little killer pay for what she'd done to me. What would my life become without her? What obsession would I enjoy next?

Vampirism paired with old age. And I was old indeed. Nearly two thousand years of existence had led me to her bed, gifting me with a happiness I never thought to experience. Then she'd shredded it and left me to exist in hell without her.

Never again.

I took another sip of my coffee, watching as Roskana and Kseniya bent their heads together, discussing their master, Jude. The E.V.I.E. director had no idea how lucky he was to have two such gifted humans in his midst.

Ah, but they weren't really humans, were they?

I hid a smile behind my cup.

Did he know about their amulets, their immortality, or their slayer bloodlines? Would he even believe it?

"Rowan," a blonde female said, approaching their table.

*Ah, yes. Rowan—Roskana's new name.* She'd kept her last name, though. *Sokolov.*

The two slayers seemed surprised to see the svelte

woman, but recognition flared in their eyes at her sensual approach. I leaned forward, intrigued by the development.

"Miranda," Roskana greeted, her tone holding a hint of distrust, something my vampiric senses picked up on as I angled my enhanced hearing in their direction.

"Jude would like to speak with you," the one called Miranda said, her voice holding a sultry lilt to it.

She had the kind of body and aura that would have captivated me a century ago.

Before I'd met Kseniya.

The little killer had ruined me for everyone else. Case in point, my erection had died the moment Miranda had arrived, all thoughts of my revenge fucking gone in a breath.

It only made me hate Kseniya more.

"Right now?" Roskana asked.

"Of course not," the blonde replied. "This evening will be fine." She refocused on Kseniya. "Don't you have somewhere to be, rather than sitting here gossiping, Violet?"

*Ugh.* I was not a fan of that chosen name. It'd taken me several days to discover Kseniya's new identity. Fortunately, the vampires kept reasonable records on the E.V.I.E. slayers.

But "Violet"? Seriously?

Sure, her hair had taken on a purple hue, but naming herself after a flower suggested a softness and innocence I knew she didn't possess.

Although, I could admire her stems in those jeans.

And she did smell rather fragrant.

I ran my thumb over the bottom of my lip, considering her as Miranda took her leave. I hadn't listened to the rest of their conversation, too caught up in my inner musings about Kseniya's nickname.

*Violet.*

*So fucking absurd.*

I would not be calling her that.

Pushing away my thoughts, I used my sensitive ears to eavesdrop on their conversation once more.

"...something in the way he handed me this assignment, Ro," Kseniya was saying. "Then casually mentioning a rumor that is so closely tied to our history? Our real history?" She leaned back in her chair and ran her long fingers through her luscious hair. It made me want to grab a fistful myself and yank her to her knees. "I think Jude knows more about us than he's let on."

Roskana sucked in a breath. "How much do you think he knows?"

*A few things,* I thought, smiling to myself.

I'd needed a way to ensure the E.V.I.E. director sent Kseniya on this mission, not some other slayer, so I'd provided some of his lapdog vampires with morsels of information I knew would be whispered back to their master. Including commentary about Kseniya's Russian ancestry.

He didn't know the full truth, just enough to intrigue. And allowing it to slip that the new ancient in town also descended from that same region made for a suitable assignment match.

It'd been a risk—one that had more than paid off.

He'd be watching.

I didn't care.

As far as I was concerned, I'd happily kill him, too. Once I finished with Kseniya.

I couldn't see her expression, as my corner booth faced her back and not her front, but I imagined she appeared disappointed or maybe even distraught by her inability to explain how Jude knew that important detail about her life.

Oh, how I longed to indefinitely carve a distraught expression of my own into her gorgeous features, to leave her in tears for decades and bathe in her sadness.

Mmm, just that thought had my groin stiffening once more.

I always did enjoy the sight of her tears.

"I wish I knew more, but that's it," she said softly. "I just wanted to warn you to watch your back."

*How touching*, I thought, gagging to myself.

And there went my intrigue.

I yanked my senses back in and left them to their heartfelt moment. It would be the final one of Kseniya's life, so I hoped she enjoyed it.

My phone began to buzz against my leg, bringing my attention to the time.

Pulling the device from my pocket, I noticed my assistant's name. "Yes?" I answered.

"Your six o'clock has just arrived," she informed me. "What should I tell them?"

"That I'm running late and will be there in about thirty minutes." I hadn't forgotten my appointment with the media. I just wanted to keep them guessing a little longer about my true identity. After all, I couldn't risk the photos circulating before Kseniya arrived. It had to be a surprise.

Would she scream and try to run? Or would she attempt to fight me?

My lips curled. I truly hoped she chose the latter. We used to have so much fun sparring together. I always went easy on her. That ended when she committed me to nearly a century of hell.

"Okay, sir. I'll let them know."

"Thank you, Gretchen," I replied, slipping my phone back into my pocket.

Kseniya and Roskana had fallen silent, consumed by their meals. Deciding it was a good time to slip out undetected, I left a reasonable tip on the table and used my mind persuasion to mask my appearance as I moved through the diner.

Neither slayer noticed, too at ease in their surroundings to even think a predator lurked among them.

*I'm disappointed*, I thought at Kseniya as I walked not five feet away from her. *I taught you better than this.*

And yet, she didn't even flinch, her guard completely down.

It would be so easy to grab that pretty little neck and snap it. But that'd be too kind, and my sweet killer deserved a more fitting demise.

*Soon*, I promised, stepping out of the diner. *Soon.*

# VIØLET

## CHAPTER FIVE

*TO WHOM IT MAY CONCERN: Evening gowns are not appropriate for midnight slaying missions.* I snapped a photo to go with my texted comment and sent it to Jude. Then I added, *I have one stake. One. And it's in my fucking handbag.*

*You look stunning,* he replied.

I glared at the screen. *Seriously? That's all you're going to say?*

Dots appeared before his reply came through. *Sorry, busy forwarding the image to the team. Talk later.*

I growled, shoving my phone back into my purse.

This was the most ridiculous mission of my existence. My kill rate was among the highest in E.V.I.E., and he wanted to waste all that skill in a slinky black gown? *Ugh.* I glared at myself in the bathroom mirror.

I'd arrived at this horrific event thirty minutes ago. They'd tried to check my purse, and I'd not so politely refused.

Refined society and I were not meant to be, something Jude had to know by now.

I preferred old bars, dungeons, and the desert. Not this high-society bullshit that required me to smile and act like a lady.

The hairdressers had hated me, mostly because anything other than a ponytail looked wrong on my head. Alas, they'd found a way to string up my purple tresses into a teased bun that appeared somewhat elegant. They'd applied ample makeup to my face, commenting on how it made my violet eyes pop.

Then they'd poured me into this tight black dress that revealed far too much cleavage and dipped so low in the back I was afraid my ass might make an appearance if I moved the wrong way.

I looked like sex on legs.

*Vampire bait.*

The heels on my feet felt wrong. They raised my five-foot-nothing height up to five foot four and were entirely impractical for slaying. The manufacturer could have at least affixed a razor-sharp end to the bottom, but no. These were purely meant for fashion purposes.

Ugh.

I took a champagne flute from a passing tray with a muttered "Thank you" and tried to melt into the background again. However, my dress made that impossible. Male eyes followed me everywhere, and females flashed me envious looks. It all left me feeling very out of my element and exposed.

Goose bumps pebbled along my limbs, leaving me with an uneasy sensation in the pit of my stomach. This wasn't my playground. I didn't know how to act here. And it reminded me of a world I left long ago.

How many parties had I attended with Roskana and Emerald? We'd been three of Anastasia's closest friends, invited to every political affair imaginable. There'd been dresses. Dances. Tempting males.

*Cassius.*

His presence taunted my memories, the way he fit a suit a visual I would never forget. Or how he looked outside of it.

I nearly groaned, my thighs clenching as they always did when I considered him.

My body refused to acknowledge his betrayal, while my heart gave a pang of agony.

*Stop thinking about him,* I told myself.

But I couldn't.

Even the colors of this fundraiser reminded me of him. All golds and reds, the colors of the Romanov Dynasty prominent and palpable. There was even a pair of golden eagles hanging over the entrance at the front of the room.

This building wasn't one I'd ever been inside before, but I sensed the fashionable décor was done for the event and not a usual theme for the room.

Deep red carpet.

Black tables.

Gold adornments.

A dance floor of obsidian marble.

I frowned. This whole atmosphere reminded me of the final ball I attended just a month before leaving my realm. Only with modern decor disguised as an otherwise obvious reference.

Was I just imagining it?

The lights above seemed to sparkle, drawing my gaze upward to the chandelier dangling from the high ceiling. A similar visual painted my memories, one holding real candles, not electric lights.

*I'm losing it,* I thought as a familiar fragrance of cinnamon twined with ginger tickled my nose. My muscles loosened, my heart thumping in my chest as I indulged my senses by inhaling deeply through my nose.

I nearly sighed.

I loved that scent.

It reminded me of Cassius's cologne.

I blinked away from the chandelier, my brow furrowing.

Something wasn't right. First Jude's mention of the Romanov link, and now all these—

"Hello, Kseniya," a deep voice said right against my ear.

The champagne glass fell from my hand, only to be caught by his as he wrapped his opposite arm around my waist.

*No.*

*It... it...*

I tried to turn around, only to be hushed by the strong male behind me as he pulled me backward into his solid frame. "Now, now, sweet slayer. It's best we not make a scene."

"Cassius," I breathed, frozen against him, my mind blanking. It was as though my thoughts had conjured him.

*Impossible.*

*He can't be here.*

*I'm imagining this.*

"Mmm," he hummed, sipping my drink before setting it on a passing tray. "I still prefer vodka, but my planner insisted that champagne would be a more suitable drink for the event." His hands found my hips, whirling me toward him.

Silver irises burned into mine, searing me to my very soul.

*It's him.*

*He's here.*

*Cassius is* here.

"Why, darling, you look as though you've seen a ghost." He sounded deeply entertained, his lips curving into one of his taunting grins. Seeing it brought back so many memories of sparring matches, all of them ending with me naked beneath him.

Not tonight.

Not now.

Not *here.*

The part of my brain that knew how to survive ignited,

sending my hand to the clutch in my opposite palm. I unsnapped it, only to feel his fingers trap mine. He plucked the purse deftly from my grip and set it on a table beside us, then grabbed my hips before I could leap away from him.

"Easy," he murmured, tugging me closer. My hands went to his shoulders, intending to shove him away as he added, "We'll fight properly later."

"*How?*" I demanded through clenched teeth, my stomach rioting with a myriad of emotions.

Terror.

Shock.

Sadness.

*Longing.*

I never thought I'd see him again. Yet here he stood, holding me at a fundraiser with a chandelier glittering over his head.

Not a thing had changed about him. He still had that stark white hair, thick and flowing past his shoulders. Piercing silver eyes. Definitive jaw structure, broad shoulders, tapered waist of solid muscle. He even smelled the same, his cinnamon scent tickling my senses.

There was no doubt in my mind that he was real. Here. *Alive.* And the hint of cruelty in his gaze told me I was the reason he'd come.

Amusement flirted with his features. "How will we fight later?" he asked, clarifying my question incorrectly. "With blood and teeth, I imagine."

"How are you here?" I reiterated.

He guided me into a dance, swaying our hips in time with the classical music playing within the room. I supposed it made us appear less conspicuous, but the intimacy of it wasn't lost on me. He held me as he did all those years ago, his body harsh and unyielding against mine. I hated how it awoke nerves long lost to another realm.

*This can't be happening.*

Only it was.

He was here.

Right fucking in front of me.

Heat engulfed me from head to toe, the desire to kill him a hot coal to my senses. However, my body refused me, my limbs moving with his as though I were a puppet beneath his control.

A hundred years.

A hundred *fucking* years.

And he still had the power to control me.

*No, no.* The amulet hanging from my neck ensured my safety. He couldn't compel me so long as I wore it.

"Did you miss me, darling slayer?" he asked softly, ignoring my question about his arrival into this realm. "Because I've missed you." He kept one arm around my lower back while his opposite palm went to my face, cupping my cheek. "I've dreamed so long of painting the room with your sweet, seductive blood. I can't wait to make that dream a reality, pet."

I shivered against him, my insides melting and solidifying and melting again.

He'd dreamt of my blood just as I'd dreamt of his. Among other things.

"The only one who is going to bleed is you," I promised him, narrowing my eyes.

The edges of his mouth curled. "So confident."

"You always underestimated me, Cassius. Look where it got you." He'd thought it would be so easy to catch me unawares and slaughter me in the middle of the night with his hungry vampire mob. Then I'd escaped because he hadn't counted on Rowan's magic being able to teleport us to a new realm.

His smile slipped into a frown. "Yes. I'm very aware of

how that turned out." The arm along my lower back turned to granite. "You won't be jumping realms again."

Now it was my turn to twist up my lips. "You say that like you can control it."

"I can," he replied, the hand on my cheek shifting to my hair. I didn't understand his intent until I felt the weight of the amulet drop into my dress. I tried to grab it, but he was faster, pocketing the item before I even had a chance to comprehend his actions.

*Vampiric speed.*

As a born slayer, I could move faster than a human, but I couldn't keep up with an ancient like Cassius.

*Ancient,* I repeated to myself. "Oh my God…" He was my target for tonight, the unknown entity in the game. I'd completely forgotten my mission the moment he whispered my name, but now it all made sense. "You set this all up." Which meant he'd been in this realm for at least a few weeks, if not longer.

*Alexander Ivanovich.*

How had I missed the obvious link?

*Cassius Alexander Ivanov.*

"Fuck," I breathed, furious with myself for not thinking this through. I'd just never thought it was possible for him to be here. Of course, I never would have thought it possible for me to be here either.

"Have you grown slower in your old age?" he asked, canting his head slightly to the side. "Perhaps a few mortal days will help."

*My amulet.*

Without it, I would be mortal. Just like he said.

I didn't ask for it back. Instead, I reached into his pocket to take it. But he caught my wrist and pulled it back up to his shoulder, holding it there with his hand over mine. "Don't," he warned when my other hand started to move.

"Or what?" I asked, ignoring his caution.

He seized my hand and spun me so quickly I nearly lost my footing in the high heels. *Damn high-society costume!*

The air whooshed out of me as my back hit his chest again. I squirmed, ready to fight, only to be caged in by Cassius's strength. He had my arms crossed in front of me beneath his own stronger ones, resembling a back hug of sorts that made me want to kill him even more.

Several eyes were on us, everyone interested in the male at my back.

Because he was the fundraising benefactor.

The supposed billionaire descending from Romanov family fame.

How had I been so naïve as to step right into this inane trap?

"I forgot how hot your anger makes me," he whispered into my ear, his nose skimming my neck to my pulse. "Mmm, you smell so fragile, love."

A growl worked its way up my throat, but I swallowed it down and took control of my features. He'd been right. We couldn't afford to create a scene here with so many humans watching us. And there would be no quiet takedown between us. It would be brutal, ugly, and savage.

"Do you still fantasize about me at night, little killer?" The words were soft and seductive, weaving a spell of history and enchanted memories through my mind. "Do you think about how I used to slay you with my cock?"

*Oh God...* My thighs clenched at the vulgar words, my heart skipping a beat in my chest. I hated how I still reacted to him after all this time. He'd betrayed me. *Hurt* me. Killed those I loved. Terminated the entire Romanov slayer line. Lusting for him was so fucking wrong yet felt so damn right.

*No. I refuse.*

*Pull yourself together!* I snapped at myself.

I was acting like a teenage slayer, lost to the whims of a sexy vampire. I'd grown so much since we'd last danced. There were parts of my mind he would never access again. Not without my permission.

"The only slaying fantasies I have are ones where I drive a stake through your cold heart," I managed to reply, my voice lacking my usual snark.

"Mmm, foreplay," he replied, nipping my pulse. "My favorite. Now be a good girl and behave for me. Maybe I'll give you back your amulet as a prize."

"You can't be ser—"

"Mister Ivanovich?" a feminine voice came from the side, followed by a beaming blonde female with a notepad in her hand. "Is this the mysterious date you teased us about?"

"It is," he said, tightening his hold in warning. "This is my fiancée, Kseniya Romanov."

*Ah, hell.* I was the Romanov link the rumors were about. How had I been so blind? And how had Jude known to assign this mission to me?

*Cassius*, I realized. He'd orchestrated all of this, including whatever information had been fed to Jude about me.

It all came together in my mind so blindingly fast that my head spun.

And then the cameras started to click.

"Smile," Cassius breathed against my ear. "Can't have the humans knowing anything's wrong, now can we?"

*I'm going to fucking kill you,* I thought, forcing my lips upward. *Just as soon as I get my amulet back.*

# CASSIUS

## CHAPTER SIX

LIGHTS FLICKERED AROUND US, everyone eager to learn more about the affluent billionaire and his purple-haired pet. Kseniya wasn't a traditional high-society beauty, but anyone paying attention could see the gorgeous charms in her features.

Of course, she was probably glowering at everyone. Which only entertained me more.

I'd planned this moment on purpose, knowing I'd need that added human presence to keep her in line. It was such a beautiful strategy that allowed me to manhandle her, show her off, and leave her helpless by my side.

"How does it feel, baby?" I asked against her ear. "To have no choice but to follow my every whim?" No one else would be able to hear me, my words pitched low for her senses alone. Besides, the others were too busy snapping photos to notice.

"Reminds me of compulsion," she muttered, her voice pitched low just like mine. "And how you used me before."

"Used you?" I repeated, chuckling under my breath. "Oh, darling. If anyone used someone, it was you using me." I lowered my lips to her neck, nipping her hammering pulse as another camera flashed. Her boss would love that image.

"So how did you meet?" Pamela asked, her pen poised

and ready. She'd been among the more eager of the reporters from earlier, so it hadn't surprised me that she'd possessed the courage to call out to me in the middle of the room.

The reporters only had thirty minutes to play. My public reason for this decision revolved around wanting to spread the word about the charity. However, the truth was that I just wanted a way to distract Kseniya from trying to kill me on sight. So far, it was working. That I held her amulet in my pocket only seemed to help matters.

"Do you want to tell the story of how we met, or shall I, darling?" I asked her softly, providing my best expression of adoration for the cameras. It was an easy thing to do when I pictured Kseniya drenched in her own blood.

"I tried to kill him," my little slayer announced in a sweet voice. "He found it amusing and decided to pursue me instead."

I laughed to hide the truth of her summary, causing several of the others to join in. Humans were so easy to manipulate. Play on their insecurities and they jumped to follow suit. However, in this case, I added a hint of compulsion to it, telling them all to ignore my drunk "fiancée" and pay attention to me instead. "The truth is, we met at a party similar to this one in Russia. It was held at Catherine Palace, wasn't it, Kseniya?"

Her shoulders stiffened at the mention of the infamous slayer palace—a palace that had been completely repurposed in our reality but seemed to be a reasonably intact tourist site in this one. Of course, she would refer to it as *Romanov Palace*.

"Somewhere like that," she managed to reply, her jaw clenched so tight I was surprised I could decipher her words. "You asked me to dance."

By "dance," she meant I taunted her into sparring with me. "I did. And I impressed you."

"Yes, you swept me off my feet," she deadpanned,

causing me to grin. Because it was true. I'd knocked her legs right out from beneath her and pinned her to the icy ground, then demanded she yield.

What a beautiful night that had been, the beginning of a new relationship.

I could almost think of it fondly, except the events that followed tainted everything that had ever transpired between us.

Kissing her neck again, I tightened my hold and met Pamela's gaze. "Everything I do is for this woman. Even this event was for her." Not a lie. And when phrased the right way, it sounded incredibly romantic.

*Aww, he loves her so much*, they would think.

They weren't wrong. I just hated her more.

"Do you support the children as well, Kseniya?" Pamela asked, referring to the charity I intended to donate all of tonight's auction funds to.

"I support life," my darling slayer replied without missing a beat. "I've always felt very strongly about prolonging the quality of existence for those who can't protect themselves."

A clever way of implying she cared about the children— which, I knew, she did—while also broadening the scope of her definition to include all mortals, regardless of age.

*How quaint.*

"We can't have children ourselves," I said, playing on the heartstrings a little. "So this is our way of giving back."

"Yes, *Alexander* is infertile," Kseniya added without missing a beat, her tone taking on a confiding note.

"Careful," I whispered against her ear, causing her to shiver. To the others, I merely smiled and waved off the comment with a casual "We all have our imperfections."

"And some of us have more than others," my little slayer quipped.

My grip around her turned bruising, silencing her.

"Well, I hope you all enjoy tonight's event," I said, taking a step backward and forcing Kseniya to come with me. "Remember, cameras are only allowed until nine. Then I ask that you take your seats and enjoy the auction with everyone else."

I spun us around before they could ask anything further, shifted Kseniya to my side, and led her toward the main dance floor. She tried to grab her bag from the table as we moved by it, but I stepped her just out of reach of the item and continued guiding her toward my desired destination.

"It'll be there when we get back," I told her.

"Assuming no one takes it," she retorted.

"We're in a room full of New York City's elite. I doubt any of them want to steal your stake."

"Maybe, but if they do, they'll have questions."

"Yes, regarding your sanity," I replied. "To which I'll inform them that it's among your many imperfections. And it would be true, considering you just pissed off an ancient vampire who already wants to kill you." Quiet words. *True* words.

"You don't appreciate me talking about your erectile dysfunction?" She raised her voice, ensuring several around us overheard her.

I released a growl of warning from my throat. "Do you require a demonstration of how well I can fuck you, darling? Because I'll happily take you into the other room to remind you of my skill set."

A pretty blush shaded her cheeks as a group of patrons turned to gape at us.

I really had no choice but to follow up on my threat now. Elite society was riddled with kinky shit. They'd get off on me dragging my errant little brat out of the room to teach her a lesson.

And those who were scandalized by it would just provide

more gossip for Kseniya's boss to hear through the media channels later.

It was a win-win scenario either way.

I flashed a conspiratorial grin at a few males as I passed. "If you'll excuse us for a bit. We'll be back for the auction."

"Like hell we will," Kseniya seethed under her breath.

"Keep talking like that and I'll spank you harder, pet."

"You can try," she shot back as I pulled her into a side room that was off-limits to the guests of the party.

Kseniya didn't waste a second, her body springing into fight mode as soon as the door shut behind us. Her fist came for my face.

I blocked her with ease, my suit much more flexible than the silky little dress she wore. She tried to kick me, only to nearly fall on her ass as a result of her heels. If she wasn't careful, she'd sprain her ankle, and without her precious little amulet, she'd end up healing like a normal human.

When I told her that, she froze.

I used the distraction to back her into the door, one of my palms on her hip, the other against the wood beside her head.

She lifted her knee toward my groin, and I blocked it with my thigh, then shifted my hand from her hip to her throat, squeezing. "Stop."

"Fuck you," she seethed.

"Is that an offer, baby?" I asked, tightening my grasp even more.

Her nails went to my grip, digging in. But a little blood didn't bother me, so I allowed her the small victory while I cut off her airway.

"I told you to behave, and you disobeyed me. Now I have to teach you a lesson."

She spat at me in response.

Releasing the door, I grabbed the ornamental

handkerchief from my front pocket and dabbed it at my face while holding her throat steady in my opposite palm.

Her eyes began to water, her face losing its color.

"It'd be so easy," I said softly, my hips aligning with hers to hold her against the door. "You're so fragile in this state. So breakable. So *human*."

She lashed out with her fingers, searching my jacket in a quick move that almost impressed me. But I was too entertained by the shock in her features to feel much else.

"Did you think I'd leave your amulet in a place you'd easily find?" I asked her, tsking. "You know me better than that, little killer."

A new emotion blossomed in her violet gaze, one that caused her pulse to sing to my vampiric senses. I inhaled the aroma, enthralled by the delectable taste of her fresh, alluring *fear*.

"Mmm," I hummed, bending to skim my nose across her pale cheek. "You have no idea how I've longed for this moment. The fantasies of killing you were all that got me through my decades of torment."

Which was why I couldn't allow it to end now.

Kseniya didn't deserve quick. Nor did I desire for it to be over in an instant. I needed time to destroy her completely.

My grip loosened just enough to allow her to inhale, and I smiled as she grimaced with her first, painful breath.

"Does it burn, baby?" I asked her, kissing her temple and pressing my lips to her ear. "Try to swallow. I want to feel you flinch against my palm."

She didn't disappoint, her heart hammering in a chaotic rhythm that caused my fangs to ache for a taste of her.

Fuck, I'd missed her.

Her nails dug into my shoulder as she tried to shove me away. I held her with ease, my strength superior to hers. Even as a Romanov slayer, I could overpower her. Especially like this, with her dressed in a fancy gown and stilettos. That wasn't how she trained. And she always relied heavily on her amulet to survive.

"I hate you," she rasped, her anger an aphrodisiac that drew a possessive growl from my throat.

"Likewise," I promised her. "But I also want you." I pressed my mouth to hers, unleashing a century of pain and longing and fury into a kiss meant to make us bleed.

Her gasp went straight to my cock. Her responding bite tightened my stomach. And the sweet metallic scent of our blending essences had my heart mimicking hers in both speed and ferocity.

She made me feel alive in a way I hadn't experienced in far too long, her body igniting a fire inside my soul that left me feeling humbled and weak. Only then her tongue touched mine, not in punishment but in exploration, and I lost myself in the tender hint of the past.

Our bodies had been created for one another. Her addictive curves to my hardness. Her strength to my dominance. Her defiance to my supremacy.

I released her neck, my fingers threading through her hair, destroying her updo. She clawed her way up my chest, her hands settling on my shoulders once more.

Just for a moment, we lost ourselves to a history neither of us could ever escape.

The demon inside me roared in victory.

My mind rebelled.

My body reveled.

My spirit fractured.

I wanted to kill her. Fuck her. Demolish her. *Keep* her.

"Stop," she snapped. But just as soon as the word left her lips, she recaptured my mouth and demanded *more*.

I gave in.

I *always* gave in.

She was the ice to my fire, the light to my dark, the stars to my night.

*Why?* I wondered. *Why does it still feel so damn good?*

As though she heard me, she moaned, long and sultry and so damn hot. Only to end the sound with her knee kicking upward toward my balls. I caught her just in time, moving to block her and shoving her up against the door again with so much force that the frame rattled. She gasped this time in pain, and I delighted in it.

Her lips were red, swollen, *used*. Blood seeped from a laceration caused by my fang, and I leaned forward to lick it from her mouth. I growled in approval, the beast inside me hungry for more.

*Not yet.*

I wanted to savor this.

"I'm going to break you, Kseniya."

"You can try." The delicious rasp of her voice made me smile.

"I'll succeed."

Her fiery purple eyes narrowed. "Give me back my amulet."

I chuckled and shook my head. "Not yet. Meet me tomorrow at noon and I'll consider it."

A muscle ticked in her jaw. "Give me back my amulet and I'll consider meeting you."

"That's not how this game works, little killer," I told her softly, leaning in to lick more blood from the wound that wasn't healing on her lips. "You want your precious immortality back, then you'll play by my rules."

"Or I'll just have Rowan make me another amulet." She sounded so sure that I would have believed her had I not known how the necklaces were made for her kind.

"Doesn't that require Romanov blood?" While Roskana could jump realms to obtain the precious essence, it wouldn't be easy. Anastasia Romanov had no memory of her past, thanks to vampire compulsion. Did Kseniya know that? Had they visited their friend?

I frowned then, considering. If they had visited Anastasia, why hadn't they tried to free her? Perhaps I wasn't the only one who'd been screwed over. It seemed odd, though. The four slayers had once been inseparable.

I nearly asked, only to have Kseniya cut off my thoughts with a snarled "If you want a fair fight, you'll give me back the amulet."

"Darling, even with it, nothing about our sparring would be fair."

"Return my necklace and we'll find out."

My lips curled. "Adorable, but no. Meet me tomorrow and maybe we'll negotiate something." I gave her an address in New York City, knowing perfectly well I wouldn't be returning her amulet anytime soon yet needing her to play along regardless.

Rather than allow her to reply, I licked the blood along her lower lip once more and abruptly stepped back to release her. "I have an auction to kick off. If you want to play nice, you're welcome to remain as my date. Or you can run along and tell your slayer friends all about me. I'm sure they would find our history entertaining."

"Cassius."

"I'm not giving you back your amulet, sweet slayer," I said, fixing my clothes and running my hand over my jacket to ensure I was all put back together. "You may want to fix your hair and makeup."

She scowled.

"Or not. I'm fine with everyone knowing I just destroyed you with my mouth." I ran my eyes over her, my nose twitching at the delicious aroma gracing her thighs. "It's a shame they won't be able to smell how much you want more."

"The only thing I want is to kill you."

"Mmm, more foreplay," I drawled. "You know how much I love a good fight to warm us both up." I winked at her and reached to pull her away from the door. "Have a good night, Kseniya. Dream of me."

I slipped out before she could reply, but I caught her angry snarl as the door swung closed behind me. I smirked, then looked at a few guests lingering a little too close to the private area. "The auction is about to begin," I informed them all, a hint of compulsion underlining my tone. "Go find your seats." *Like good humans*, I added in my mind.

The lambs all did my bidding, turning without so much as a *baa* in reply.

That was what I adored about Kseniya. She would never listen, just as I knew she wouldn't now. I anticipated her walking back out with her head held high and smiled as she stepped through the threshold right on cue.

She didn't even look at me. Just proceeded toward the table to collect her bag and then went straight to the exit with her tousled hair still a mess on her head.

*That's my girl*, I thought after her. Then I flagged Gretchen over with a wave.

"Yes, sir?" she asked, her dark hair perfectly pinned on top of her round head.

"I need to attend to something important," I told her. "Can you apologize on my behalf to the guests and run the auction without me? We can provide them all with a bottle of the finest champagne as a consolatory gift."

Her ebony eyes told me she wanted to argue, but the intelligent woman knew better. "Of course, sir. Do you need my assistance with anything else?"

"Just tonight's benefit," I replied. "See that everything

runs smoothly in my absence, and I'll add a substantial bonus to your next check."

She didn't react gluttonously to the news, merely bowed her head. "Thank you, sir."

"Call me after with an update."

"Yes, sir."

"Thank you, Gretchen," I said, taking my leave without a single glance back. I couldn't give two fucks about this entire room of society imbeciles and their flagrant displays of money. The only reason I'd shown up was for Kseniya, and as she'd left early, so would I.

Without her amulet, she was breakable—a state I intended to exploit personally. That didn't mean I wanted anyone else to harm her.

So I followed her to the flat she kept in Upper Manhattan.

She never once thought to look for me. It had me shaking my head in disapproval. The vampires in this realm were too easy to kill, allowing her to forget everything I'd ever taught her.

We'd speak more about it tomorrow.

After she found the present I had planned for her.

My mouth twitched in amusement. We'd just entered phase one of our game. I hope she was ready, or it'd end before it truly began.

*Good night, little killer. Sweet dreams.*

# CHAPTER SEVEN

I WAS WRONG.

Jude didn't call me at all. Instead, he showed up at nine o'clock in the morning with Luci beside him and a newspaper in his hand. I knew what would be on that paper before he even said a word.

Given that I'd only slept a few hours after fretting most of the night, I had no energy to argue with him or deflect his questions. Rather than try, I just opened my door, allowed him to enter, and went straight to the coffee maker.

I poured us both a cup on autopilot, added the appropriate fixings, and took the chair across from him at my dining room table.

Luci wandered over to nudge me with her snout, her big eyes filled with concern. "I'm okay," I promised her.

A lie.

I wasn't *okay* at all.

*Cassius is here. In New York City. In our current realm.*

I'd tried to call Rowan to tell her, but she hadn't answered her phone. For whatever reason, her voicemail hadn't worked, so I decided I'd ring her back today. After I met with Cassius again.

My plan was simple: get my amulet back and kill him.

Of course, I wasn't so naïve as to expect him to go along

with that. And not having my amulet would prove to be dangerous because if anyone could best me, it was Cassius. Just as he'd done last night.

Jude slid the paper across the table, the photo displaying Cassius kissing my neck as he held me tight against him. "When I asked you to gather intelligence, I meant for you to hide on the sidelines and observe."

"You dressed me as vampire bait," I scoffed. "What did you expect?" I supposed that worked as a nice deflection. But I could see in Jude's eyes that he knew I wasn't telling him the truth, and his follow-up question proved it.

"Who is he, Violet?" The serious lines of his face demanded compliance with that inquiry. Telling a version of the truth wasn't going to fly. As I had questions for him, too, I figured we might as well get it all out in the open.

"How did you know the Romanov tie would interest me into taking the case?" I countered him. "Why not give the project to Alaric or one of the others? Why me?"

"You know why."

"I *suspect* why," I corrected. "I want you to confirm it."

"Come on, *Kseniya*. Let's not dance around the truth. Tell me who Alexander Ivanovich is to you. Is he from your home realm?"

That question alone confirmed he knew Rowan and I weren't from this reality but from another. "How long have you known?"

"Stop deflecting."

"It's relevant," I argued. "I'm trying to figure out how you found out. Was it through rumor? Observation? Did someone tell you about my true identity?"

His eyes narrowed. "It was through a mixture of observation, my predecessor's notes regarding your amulet, and a rumor trickling around about your ties to the Romanov Dynasty. I put it all together and decided to test a theory." He gestured to the photo in the paper with his chin. "That proves said theory. Who is he?"

I ran my palm over my face and sighed. "Have you spoken to Rowan yet?"

"I've answered enough questions. Your turn."

"So that's a no," I muttered. Which of course it was. Had he told Rowan, she'd have shown up with him. "His name is Cassius Alexander Ivanov. He's a vampire, but not the kind you're used to slaying."

"Go on," he encouraged when I paused to think about how difficult it would be to take out Cassius. Wanting him dead and killing him were two entirely different sentiments.

"He's immune to sunlight, garlic, stakes, and pretty much every other manner taught by the E.V.I.E. trainers. You wondered why I never desired more instruction? It's because the vampires in this realm are child's play compared to what Rowan and I dealt with back home." There was no sugarcoating it. This realm was a complete joke compared to the reality we came from.

Pushing away from my chair, I went to grab a blanket to wrap around my bare shoulders. Suddenly the tank top and shorts I wore were just too revealing for the story I needed to tell.

Jude didn't push, his dark eyes guarded as I re-collected myself on the chair again.

And then I told him everything.

Because why bother hiding it? He knew enough already that it didn't hurt to share the truth about my lineage as Anastasia's distant cousin. Rowan was a cousin of a different sort, as her family was meant to protect those of the Romanov line.

"That's why we have the amulets," I explained. "One of the key markers is blood from a direct descendant of the Romanov line. Such as Anastasia. So, unfortunately, Rowan can't make more because the entire family is dead." I added that last bit to keep him from garnering any ideas on how to use my oldest friend to create an army of immortal slayers.

Then I went into the history of that night and how the Romanov slayer line ended.

Which brought me to Cassius and his infamous cousin. *Dimitri.*

"The Romanovs had a tenuous alliance with the Vampire Dynasty after their king, Dimitri Ivanov, stated his desire to find a meaningful coexistence between our houses."

I thought back on those days of wistful hope. While I'd been young, just twenty years old and freshly trained in the art of slaying, there'd been a sort of quiet peace that had hung among the Romanovs and the families of those who supported our cause.

Everyone had been at war for so long. They were exhausted and beaten down and more than eager to accept the pause that allowed them to negotiate a new way forward.

"Dimitri lied," I whispered.

My eyes fell closed, the nightmare rolling through my mind in a hot memory that singed my senses.

"His vampires burned the Romanov Palace—which is similar to your current Catherine Palace just outside of Saint Petersburg—and the surrounding grounds to ash." I swallowed, recalling the flames and heat from that night. "Someone led them through the secret tunnels, right into the heart of our territory. No one had expected them. No one had stood a chance."

It'd been Cassius who'd led them.

I still recalled seeing his white hair glistening in the embers, his eyes wild as he searched for me.

"Rowan saved my life." I purposely left out Emerald, the other slayer Rowan had saved. I didn't want to bring our rebellious sister into this. She'd chosen her destiny as a non-slayer, and I respected that choice. "We've tried to go back so many times. But I guess your reality needed us more."

Luci put her head on my thigh, her big eyes filled with love and affection. I set my hand on her soft neck, then ran my fingers through her silky fur, scratching her behind the ears and along her nape.

"I suppose you needed me, too, hmm?" I said to her, smiling.

She didn't exactly grin back, but her eyes spoke right to my soul. *Yes.*

"I've known for a while that your amulets let you travel through portals," Jude admitted after a few minutes. "I suspected it was also tied to your immortality since neither of you has aged a day since we first met, and my predecessor has information reflecting the same fact."

"We weren't exactly hiding it."

"No, you weren't," he agreed. "So why not come clean about your origin?"

I blew out a long breath, considering all the reasons Rowan and I had decided not to talk about it with anyone in this realm. Emerald was at the top of that list, our desire to safeguard her identity of utmost importance. If E.V.I.E. learned about her existence and some of her rarer traits, they'd recruit her in a heartbeat. And Emerald would not react well.

However, beyond that, we'd worried about Jude wanting Rowan to create more amulets. They took so much out of her and were impossible to complete without blood from a direct Romanov descendant.

We suspected mine might be enough, if I provided ample amounts of it, but we hadn't experimented, because it could put my own life in jeopardy.

But it was more about the toll it took on Rowan.

Neither of us wanted her to be used or forced to create something that left her so weak and powerless.

I chewed the inside of my cheek, debating how to phrase that without offending Jude. "We weren't sure how you'd react," I finally decided upon. "It's something we can't fix or take back, and we never expected our old world to find us. We've been here since 1918."

"Well, your past has caught up with you," he returned.

"Obviously." I cleared my throat, biting back the series of curses I wanted to add to that statement. This wasn't Jude's fault. Nor was it mine. "Cassius and I have history. I suspect he started whatever rumors you heard about me. It's the only way he could have guaranteed you'd give me the invitation to the fundraiser last night."

"So he's been killing indiscriminately to garner your attention," Jude translated.

I frowned. "That... I think might be a coincidence."

"Coincidence?" he scoffed. "It all started at the same time. Without the dead bodies, there would have been no need to attend last night."

I shook my head. "No, you would have wanted someone to go to check out the new ancient. Spreading a rumor about his age and status is something Cassius would do. Kill without cause... that doesn't feel like him."

Jude arched a dark brow. "Did you not just tell me a story about his brethren slaughtering the Romanov slayer line?"

"That was Dimitri's call," I pointed out. "And it was to end a feud between slayers and vampires that went back centuries." An entirely different situation, despite the bloodshed involved.

"Over a hundred years ago," Jude said. "Who knows what your old reality looks like now, Violet?"

A fair comment. However... "It's not his usual methodology. Planning a lavish affair and coaxing me out by dropping hurtful reminders of my past is what I expect from him. He gains nothing by killing the humans."

I wasn't sure why I felt the need to defend him. For all I knew, he was the idiot slaying aimlessly in the street. But my gut told me it wasn't him, that it was all just a coincidental occurrence.

Cassius wanted to fuck with me.

He couldn't give a shit about everyone else.

*That* was the vampire I knew.

"The scenes were too messy," I added.

"Again, a lot can change in a century," Jude said softly. "Perhaps that's how it's done in your world now."

I flinched at the thought, my stomach tightening with a rage that boiled my blood. What if Rowan and I were wrong about our fate? What if we weren't meant to be in this reality, but in our own, and we'd wasted the last hundred or so years working for the wrong team?

My coffee was suddenly too cold to drink. Not that I'd really touched it since sitting down.

"Where's your amulet?" Jude asked suddenly, gazing at my neck. I suspected he'd been checking me for bites, only to realize my trademark chain was missing.

"Cassius took it." I sounded far more defeated than I intended, but I'd stayed up all night thinking about his reappearance in my life and how to handle it. "I'm supposed to meet him at noon." I told Jude the place and shook my head. "I don't know what he has planned, but he's not just going to give me my amulet back. He knows what it does."

"Why is he fixated on you?"

"Because I escaped him," I replied.

His eyes narrowed. "It's more than that."

I lifted a shoulder. "His reasoning is irrelevant. He's here, he wants to kill me, and I'm not going to let him. So I have to meet him at noon even though I know it won't be that simple."

Jude nodded. "You'll take Alaric with you."

"What? No, he—"

"Did I phrase that as a request?" Jude gave me a look that told me I knew damn well he wasn't going to allow me to argue.

"This is my fight, Jude."

"And you'll get it, with Alaric as backup."

"No offense to Alaric, but he won't stand a chance against Cassius." He was a human with impressive strength and speed, I'd give him that. However, Cassius resembled a god in this world, one I could barely take down with my hardened slayer heritage.

Jude's lips twitched. "You know, for as observant as you can be, you certainly overlook certain details."

"What the hell does that mean?"

He lifted a shoulder. "I'm not going to spell it out for you, but I'll tell Alaric to be in that restaurant by half past eleven."

"No."

"It's not a debate, Violet. He'll be assisting you with or without your permission."

My teeth ground together in frustration. "Jude, you don't know Cassius like I do."

"I'm aware of that. I'm also aware that he makes you uneasy, something I've never known you to be. And he was able to one-up you by taking your amulet." Jude stood, his coffee mug empty. "You'll be accepting Alaric's help, Violet. He's more resourceful than you're giving him credit for."

"It's not that. I just…" I trailed off, palming the back of my neck. "I don't want him to get hurt because of me."

"Then prepare him," Jude suggested. "I'll have him come here first. You can brief him on Cassius and develop a plan."

Fuck.

He wasn't going to listen to me regardless, which left me no choice but to nod in acceptance. At least with my acquiescence, I could help prepare Alaric on what we were about to face. Maybe I could even convince him to bow out of the mission.

Yes, that was what I would do.

I'd scare him off.

Then handle Cassius myself.

# Violet

## CHAPTER EIGHT

My plan to dissuade Alaric went up in flames almost as soon as it started. He had no qualms about meeting a vampire from another universe.

"It's about time fate gave me a decent challenge," he'd said with a grin. Then he'd left my apartment with a skip in his step, eager to face my immortal god of an ex-lover. I'd warned him repeatedly not to act without me. I just hoped he listened to my advice.

*Ugh. Today sucks.*

I'd called Rowan to give her a quick rundown of my meeting with Jude as well. She'd been more concerned with Cassius being back than with Jude finding out about our history. Apparently, they'd engaged in a cryptic conversation while I was pampering for my event, one that had indicated to her that he knew more than he'd let on.

Well, now he knew everything.

Except for the part about my intimate history with Cassius.

It'd been hinted at enough for Jude to connect the dots. He didn't need to know more because it wouldn't matter after today.

Cassius would be dead.

I'd have my amulet back.

All would be sane in the world once more.

Except, as Rowan had pointed out, I needed to know more about how Cassius had traversed the realms. On the one hand, it implied we might have a way to finally go home. On the other hand, it suggested more vampires might be coming for us.

Neither of us was sure how to interpret it, and there hadn't been enough time for us to do a deep dive. By the time Rowan had finished freaking out about Cassius and what it meant for me, Alaric was knocking at my door. Which was why I hadn't told her about my amulet, either. As I intended to retrieve it today, it wasn't a big deal.

"All right, Luci," I said, looking at the fluffy tangle of fur on the couch. "Time to go."

Her brown eyes peered up at me like I'd lost my mind.

"What? You don't want to help me slay today?" I asked her.

She yawned in response and closed her eyes.

I arched a brow. "But you like vampire bones."

No response.

Not even a twitch.

"I see." Hades must have exhausted her with their overnight playdate. "Then I'll just go out and handle Cassius myself."

Well, with Alaric's assistance.

He was supposed to arrive ten minutes before me. Knowing him, he was already there.

With a sigh, I left my preferred companion behind to nap on the couch and took off toward the address Cassius had given me. I was nearly there when my phone rang, Alaric's number flashing on the screen.

Frowning, I answered. "Don't tell me you already killed him."

"Not quite," he replied. "Where are you?"

"About a block away."

"Good. Because we have a problem."

"What kind of problem?" I asked, picking up my pace.

"A dead-body kind of problem," he muttered, hanging up before I could ask for details.

I blinked at the screen, then slid my phone into my pocket and took off at a jog down the street toward the deli. Alaric met me at the door, his eyebrows pinched. "The place was dark when I arrived because it's not open on the weekends."

I glanced at the dark windows, noting the lack of people. "So you broke in?"

"Yeah." He cleared his throat. "I could, uh, smell the corpse. Well, corpses."

My nose twitched as I inhaled. "You could smell it?"

He nodded, stepping out of the way to let me inside. "Try not to touch anything. Jordan is on his way, and you know how particular he can be."

I didn't move. "What do you mean, you could smell it?"

"You want to debate nuances of how I sensed death lurked here? Really?" He arched a brow. "Don't you think it's a little more important to go in and see the gifts your vampire left for you?"

Well, he had a point there. But Jude's words from earlier about me overlooking details had me evaluating Alaric in a new light. *Who smells corpses?* I supposed if the odor was strong enough, it would have wafted into the street. And knowing what I did about New York City, not many humans would take notice of it. Or care, for that matter.

"Did you have to disable an alarm?" I wondered out loud as I stepped over the threshold into the small deli.

"Yeah. I did that before breaking the lock."

I glanced over my shoulder at him. "And you broke the lock, how?"

He huffed a laugh. "Come on, Vi. It's me."

*True.* He had a gadget for pretty much everything.

"Any other trivial questions you want to ask before we focus on what really matters here?" he asked, arching a brow again.

"Jude says I don't pay enough attention to you," I said, looking over his tight T-shirt and jeans. "I'm trying to figure out what he meant."

"That you should fuck me, probably."

I grunted. "Pretty sure that's not it."

"Pretty sure you'd enjoy it, though," he tossed back.

"Oh, we both know I would." I smiled at him. "Just as we both know it'll never happen."

"No mixing business with pleasure," he drawled.

"*Precisamente, amor.*"

He rolled his eyes. "Stop fucking around and get to work."

"Yes, sir." I mock-bowed, then concentrated on the crime scene. Or as Alaric had called it, the "gifts" Cassius had left for me.

All the humor provoked by my conversation with Alaric died upon seeing the remains of three bodies tossed haphazardly into a corner.

A chill swept through me.

*So wrong.*

*So harsh.*

*So... messy?*

There was blood everywhere, painting the walls, the counter, and the floor. I took it all in with a frown, my mind trying to process the brutality before me.

"This doesn't make any sense." Cassius would never be so clumsy with a kill, let alone allow so much of the life essence to go to waste.

"Does death ever make sense?" Alaric countered.

"No, I mean the scene. This isn't Cassius." I was certain of it.

Alaric moved to stand beside me, his expression incredulous. "How does he usually kill, then?"

"Not like this," I said, gesturing to the mess of tangled limbs and remains. "He would never waste all this blood, and he wouldn't leave the bodies in such a careless position either. Actually, none of this feels like him. It's too… *loud*. Like the predator is trying to make a statement."

While I knew Cassius had a lot to say, this wasn't it. What did he have to gain by leaving a bunch of dead humans for me to find? He wanted me dead. To destroy *me*. Slaying mortals wouldn't accomplish that.

"This isn't him," I said again. "But he clearly knew this would be here." I went to my haunches to evaluate the massacre without touching it, careful not to touch the blood splatter with my shoes. "Which means he knows who we're hunting. This is his way of giving us a clue." Suggesting that something about this scene would lead us to the next set of hints. "He loves to play games."

We used to indulge in them all the time. He'd leave me little puzzles to solve that usually concluded with me finding him waiting for me at the end. My heart gave a pang at the memory and the cruel way he took advantage of it now.

"He wants me to suffer," I whispered, more to myself than to Alaric.

Cassius desired to throw our past in my face.

To burn me in the worst way.

To confirm that everything between us had always been a lie, one he'd used to manipulate me countless times.

I'd never meant anything to him.

I knew that, but to have it thrown so harshly in my face gave me momentary pause, darkening my soul that much more.

"So you two have history," Alaric surmised. "You failed to mention that during the briefing."

"Because it's irrelevant." A complete lie. But I hadn't expected Cassius to create a new game. That'd been an intimate thing between us, a way to test my slayer skills with a treat waiting for me at the finish line.

I supposed Cassius's death could be considered a treat.

Because that was what he would be when I found him again—*dead*.

"Seems pretty fucking relevant to me," Alaric retorted. "So what clue has he left for us? What game are we playing? And if he wasn't the one who killed all these humans, who was?"

"I think that's what he wants us to find out. Cassius knows who's creating the mess, and dangling the carrots for us to follow. He probably even ensured the papers found out about Valaria Crimson's death, too." Maybe he'd even orchestrated her to be a victim. At this point, anything was possible. But I knew one thing for sure. "He's not the one killing these humans. He just knows who it is."

He could be motivating the vampire as well. Except, that didn't feel right either. Cassius was all for keeping his existence a secret. At least in his realm. Did he care less about this realm because he didn't intend to stay?

Did that mean he knew how to get back?

I stood again, more determined than ever to locate the clue he'd left. The faster we solved the puzzle, the quicker I found him.

Alaric said something, but I ignored him, searching, my mind whirring with ideas.

Memories echoed in my thoughts, all tainted by the night Cassius had tried to kill me. Blood seeped through my mind. Fire. *Darkness*.

The positioning of the bodies was too tangled to mean

anything. The bite marks were all in different locations, as though the fiend had lost himself to the gluttony of mortal conquests.

No pattern.

No logic.

Just sinful indulgence.

There had to be something here for me to find, some sort of hint. Yet the more I looked, the less it all made sense.

Had I lost sight of my skills over the last century? Grown complacent in this new world of easy kills? Or had Cassius just become that good at crafting his puzzles?

I shook my head, lost. "I don't see anything other than a messy kill." Was there a note outside? An arrow? A misplaced stone? Ignoring Alaric once more, I wandered through the door, peering up and down the sidewalk, wondering if Cassius stood someplace nearby watching me fail. Was he laughing even now? Amused by my ineptitude?

A growl worked its way up my throat, frustration visceral and harsh against my senses.

Why bother indulging me in a game if he didn't want to make it playable?

Or had that been the point? To deliver me an endless riddle of nonsense to try and fail to solve?

Maybe this wasn't a game at all, but a way to make me suffer even more. Because Cassius knew how I felt about the notion of failure.

I *never* failed.

"What about this?" Alaric said suddenly, his deep baritone yanking me from my thoughts and forcing me to look at him. To *see* him. He held out a white business card with his gloved hands, causing my brow to furrow.

The E.V.I.E. investigative unit had arrived during my perusal, and I'd been completely oblivious to them. Alaric must have gotten the gloves from them.

Rather than ask for my own, I leaned forward to read the inscription across the pale card stock. "Blood Thirteen," I read out loud. Beneath it was tomorrow's date and an evening hour. "What's Blood Thirteen?"

"A new nightclub over in Brooklyn," one of the techs replied from inside the deli, an infrared lamp in his hand. "It's invite only at the moment, but it's trending as the hot new thing."

*Hot new thing*, I thought with a snort, walking back through the threshold. Alaric followed, shutting the door behind us to keep the public from seeing the crime scene.

"Where'd you find the card?" I asked Alaric.

"Inside that one's pocket." He gestured to the blond guy on top of the pile. "I was looking for an ID and found this instead."

Of course it was that simple.

*Come on, Kseniya. You're better than this*, I chastised myself. Emotions were obviously messing with my ability to think clearly. Perhaps coupled with the rough night of sleep I'd endured as a result of Cassius's unexpected arrival.

My whole world had gone to hell in a handbasket in the blink of an eye.

All because of an immortal god of a man who had somehow found his way back into my life.

The shock had unnerved me, and that kiss last night had rendered me stupid.

Why had I even allowed him to touch me?

Oh, but I hadn't *allowed* a damn thing. He'd bested me, just like he always did.

"Did you find anything else?" I asked, forcing my mind to shut the hell up so I could pay attention to the situation at hand.

"Not yet." Alaric set the card in an evidence bag and continued working through the scene with the techs. I followed along and started to feel a bit more like myself toward the end of our analysis.

Until I remembered the clue and the man who had likely left it for us to follow.

"So it sounds like you and I have another date tomorrow. Assuming this is an invite?" Alaric stripped off his gloves. "Shall I pick you up around eight and see if they'll let us in?"

I wanted to tell him no, to say I'd handle it alone. But after my show today, it was astoundingly apparent that I couldn't deal with this on my own. My heart was too involved and clouding my ability to see properly.

*Fucking Cassius.*

"Tomorrow at eight," I managed to say, my throat thick with some convoluted mixture of anger and sadness.

Why? Why did he have to be here now? Why did he have to come for me?

"Wear something hot," Alaric murmured. "Maybe it'll distract your admirer."

I snorted at that. "Trust me, he's not an admirer."

"Well, it's certainly something, Vi. To go through all this effort for a *game*, as you called it, suggests quite an infatuation."

"We have history," I muttered. "Dark history." Understatement of the century, but I didn't want to go into it. "I'll see you tomorrow at eight." I started toward the door, then paused to look at him. "Let me know when they declare the official time of death."

We'd briefly discussed it during the initial review of the scene with the techs, but we only knew enough to say the bodies had been there for at least twelve hours. The information implied that Cassius could have been the murderer. However, I suspected the report would confirm that the deaths occurred during the fundraiser, likely at the exact time Cassius had been seen talking to me.

It would be just like Cassius to have a firm alibi, thereby supporting my theory of his presumed innocence. But I wanted to be sure.

A century was a long time. Perhaps his methods had changed. Although, given the fact that he was almost two thousand years old, I doubted a hundred years would do much.

Alaric promised to keep me informed, and I headed back to my single-bedroom condo. It was one I'd owned for about a decade now, mostly used for stopover missions such as this one.

Unfortunately, that meant I didn't have much food in the fridge. I only kept the place stocked with coffee and some other essentials. And considering how lethargic I felt climbing the three flights of stairs to my place, I really needed more than some peanuts and a caffeine boost. I'd just grab Luci and portal...

"Ugh," I grumbled to myself. I couldn't even do that because Cassius had my amulet. *Damn it!*

Stomping the rest of the way to my flat, I put the key in the door and found it already unlocked. My brow furrowed. Had I forgotten to lock up before I left? I wasn't exactly feeling like myself today, so maybe.

The door opened before I had a chance to consider my next move.

Cassius stood on the other side with a glass of red wine, his lips curled into a taunting grin. "Welcome home, darling. Long day?"

# CASSIUS

## CHAPTER NINE

KSENIYA DIDN'T EVEN BLINK, pulling a gun so fast I would have missed it had I not been looking forward to the reaction.

I caught the barrel with my free hand, yanking it from her and tucking it into my belt before grabbing hold of her neck and dragging her inside. Her curse came out as a whoosh of air as I slammed her up against the wall beside the entry. I used my heel to quickly shut the door, closing us inside.

Her nails dug into my exposed forearm, her knee flying upward in the direction of my groin. I blocked her with my thigh, then pinned her legs with mine against the wall. She was welcome to draw as much blood as she wanted with those vicious claws. I had her by the throat. She'd pass out eventually.

I sipped my wine casually while I watched her face drain of color, then canted my head to the side. "You've gotten too comfortable, sweetheart," I chastised her softly. "Without the amulet, you're very breakable. *Weak.* You require regular food now, just like a normal human. And not only did you skip breakfast today, but you also failed to eat lunch."

Her eyes widened, her lips parting on words that required access to air that she didn't possess.

I watched for a moment, enjoying her defenseless position

and the art of death creeping up on her senses. "So beautiful," I whispered, infatuated with this look on her.

Alas, it was much too soon. We had so much fun to engage in with one another before I allowed her life to end.

Just as her eyes began to flutter, I released her, then smiled at the wheeze of her inhale. "Try to shoot me again and I'll knock you out."

Leaving her to recover in the foyer, I returned to the kitchen to continue my meal preparations. The fridge had lacked proper ingredients, so I'd taken it upon myself to have several delivered. Including a raw steak for the black wolflike creature in the living room.

*A hellhound*, I mused, having finally grasped the type of animal that had followed Kseniya around with such loyalty. I hadn't gotten close enough to her to realize her true breed until now. Such a beautiful creature, something I'd told her after breaking into Kseniya's residence.

The hellhound had been disgruntled at first, her snarl one that had made my lips twitch. But the moment she met my gaze, she'd sat down and canted her head in a curious way. She'd recognized me, confirming her intelligence. I'd spoken to her quite a bit while preparing dinner.

Her shrewd gaze suggested she'd understood every word, including my threats to kill her master. Yet she hadn't done a damn thing to try to stop me, something I found fascinating.

For such a loyal animal, I'd expected a fight. Instead, she'd just returned to the couch to lie lazily along the cushions. I'd rewarded her with a raw steak.

"Luci?" Kseniya rasped, her hand around her throat as she made her way into the kitchen, murder in her expression.

"Is that your little hellhound's name?" I asked, glancing at her from the stove.

A snort from the living area confirmed it for me.

I peeked around the wall toward the couch and found the

beast giving me a lopsided grin with her tongue hanging out the side of her mouth.

"Hmm," I hummed, then went back to the stove.

Kseniya pushed past me to check on the hellhound herself, then scowled upon returning. "Did you compel her?" she asked, her voice scratchy and somewhat painful to the ears.

I turned toward the now fully stocked fridge and pulled out a bottle of water for her. "Drink that."

"Fuck you."

"Oh, we'll get to that," I promised, setting the water on the counter beside her. "And no, I didn't compel her." I nearly scoffed at the notion. The thought hadn't even crossed my mind.

"Sure," she muttered, her tone riddled with disbelief.

"Go check on her again," I suggested. *Since clearly your first glance wasn't sufficient enough*, I thought, mentally rolling my eyes.

*Compel a hellhound.*

*Right.*

Kseniya left the kitchen with a huff. I smiled when I heard her trying to stealthily open one of the drawers in the living room.

"I already found it," I called to her. I'd scoured her flat for weapons soon after arriving and had secured every possible item that could be used against me. However, I hadn't patted her down completely, which left a very strong possibility that she possessed a few blades or another gun.

I sort of hoped she did.

A sparring match would serve both of us well.

She returned a moment later, her expression giving nothing away as she opened the fridge to peruse the contents. Then she went to the pantry door, grunted, and looked at the new cooking utensils I'd acquired for tonight's meal. "Are you moving in?" she demanded.

"Would you like me to?" I countered, smirking at her.

She just grumbled an unflattering remark and picked up the water to guzzle half the contents.

"You're mortal now," I reminded her yet again. "You'll need to drink and eat regularly."

"Your concern is touching," she deadpanned.

"Oh, I'm not concerned, darling. I just want you to last long enough for me to enjoy destroying you." I plucked a handful of spices from the cupboard—all ones I'd procured for this meal—and added them to the tomato sauce simmering in the pot. Then I went back to preparing the chicken.

She watched my every move, the exhaustion in her expression holding a touch of wariness and a heavy dose of confusion.

"What did you think of my present?" I asked as I flipped the meat in the skillet. It was almost done, just like the garlic bread in the oven. I thought it'd be a fun play on the differences between a real vampire and those she'd spent the last century hunting.

"You didn't kill those humans," she replied, surprising me. I'd expected a lot of comments from her, but not that one.

"Of course I didn't." I frowned at her. "Why the hell would I?"

"But you wanted me to find them."

"Clearly."

"Because you know who the killer is and you want to taunt me with that knowledge."

I stopped stirring the sauce to gaze down at her. "Actually, I don't know who your sloppy murderer is, but he's become quite the nuisance. He started up his antics around the time I arrived, painting me as a suspect among the vampires in this region. Fortunately, they've since seen reason. I have no desire to provoke a wolf pack."

I shuddered at the very thought.

The shifters of this world weren't well known, but I gathered they were at least somewhat similar to the ones back in our home realm. And the last thing I wanted was to start a war with a bunch of angry wolves.

"Wolf pack?" she repeated, her brow furrowing.

"Yeah." I returned to my task on the stove, then checked the oven. "I found those bodies yesterday and thought you might want to check them out. They had the stench of your culprit all over them. Maybe they'll give you some sort of clue." It'd been a natural thing to point her in the right direction. Mostly because it left her in my debt, something I very much desired.

Crippling an enemy who also felt indebted to me would create the most bittersweet end.

I nearly sighed at the thought.

Then went back to finishing up our dinner.

"Why would you help me?" she asked, sounding uncertain.

"Because I can," I replied, refusing to give her more. "Go set the table."

To my surprise, she obeyed, fetching the plates and some silverware, and even taking my wine glass and her water bottle over. It was a tiny little table just off to the side of the kitchen. I doubted she used it much, as it was tucked into a corner with outdated lighting. Her living area at least had windows.

I suspected her place in Chicago was nicer, but hadn't ventured inside it. I hadn't wanted to risk her sensing me at all, therefore choosing to stick to the shadows all those months I'd watched her. It was almost a relief to finally talk to her.

Because it meant I was that much closer to my goal.

Not because I'd missed her.

She said nothing as I decorated the table with food. Nor did she try to serve herself, so I made up a plate for her of pasta, sauce, chicken, vegetables, and garlic bread on the side. When I finished, I crafted my own, then leaned back in my chair to study her position across from me.

"Eat," I told her.

A muscle ticked in her jaw. "Why?"

"Because you need to," I said, noting her trembling shoulder. "You're a Romanov by blood, which makes you stronger and more resilient than an ordinary human. But you're not a pure Romanov."

Kseniya was Anastasia Romanov's third cousin, which made her a descendant with enhanced physical attributes. However, only those in the primary line—or those among mixed slayer family lines—maintained all the gifts of a true slayer. So while Kseniya's father was a purebred, her mother had been a mere human. Which made my little killer a hybrid of sorts.

"You still have weaknesses—weaknesses you seem to have forgotten through reliance on your amulet." I tsked at her. "The Kseniya I knew never would have allowed such a slip in her training."

"The Kseniya you knew was reborn when she accidentally teleported to this realm with no way back," she snapped. "Oh, and why did that happen? Because *your kind* destroyed the palace."

"Accidentally teleported?" I repeated, arching a brow. Was that the story she intended to tell?

She waved a hand at that. "Portal-jumped. Whatever you want to call it." She leaned forward. "How did you get here?"

"How did you?" I countered.

"Rowan. I think." She shook her head. "Just tell me—do you know how to go back?"

"Of course I do." I glared at her. "Now eat your damn food."

"Are you just saying that?"

"No, I very much mean it. If you don't take a bite, I'll feed you myself, and trust me, Kseniya, you won't like that at all."

"I mean about going back. You can do it?"

"Stop derailing the subject and *eat.*" I laced that final word with a hint of compulsion.

Her pupils flared in response, her anger palpable. "Bastard." Even while she said it, her fork worked to twirl around some noodles and sauce, bringing it to her alluring mouth.

I smiled as she chewed and swallowed. "Good girl."

She flipped me off and ate more, my compulsion weaving through each of her movements, forcing her to comply. My stubborn little slayer would rather argue with me than take care of herself, so I'd do the honors for her.

The bruises surfacing around her neck contradicted my assessment, but only slightly.

When she'd finished half her plate, I allowed my compulsion to wane. However, she kept eating, her own hunger having taken over.

So I joined her in enjoying the meal. It was a bit heavy on the onion, something I blamed on the spices I'd procured. The Americans in this realm really took pleasure in their salt as well, a fact I didn't particularly favor in terms of food preparation.

Twenty minutes of contented silence passed between us. As Kseniya neared the end of her bottle, I stood to retrieve her two more, setting them before her without a word. Then

I topped off my wine. I would have offered her some, but I knew from experience that she didn't care for the substance. The only alcohol she ever indulged in was vodka—a Romanov family favorite.

She set her fork down, her plate clear.

I followed suit, watching as the color returned to her cheeks.

*Much better*, I thought, pleased to see her well fed and rejuvenated once more. "Tell me how you 'accidentally teleported,'" I said, curious to hear the lie she'd crafted.

"Tell me how to go back," she countered.

"As if you don't know," I chided. "Really, Kseniya. You'll have to do better than that."

"Do you think I'd ask you about it if I knew how to do it?"

"I think you would, yes." I smiled. "You want to know if there's another way to make the portal now that you lost your amulet."

She blinked at me. "The amulet can take us home?"

I rolled my eyes. "You're not fooling me, darling."

"How?" she asked, her expression a brilliant mask of curiosity. It was almost to the point that I believed she didn't really know. But I wasn't naïve enough to fall for such a trick. She'd known how to return for a century but just hadn't bothered to. Because she'd left me to suffer.

"Tell me, did you enjoy knowing what happened that night?" I asked her, curious. "Did you ever think about what was being done? How he intended to torture those he kept alive?"

Naturally, I was referring to Grigori. The bastard who had caught all of Dimitri's loyalists within the Romanov Palace walls, killing most of them on sight. Saving others, like me, for a worse fate.

She growled at me. "I think about that night almost every day."

"Do you regret it?" I wondered out loud, knowing that she didn't.

Tears glistened in her depths. "What do you want, Cassius? To torture me more than you already have?"

My eyebrows lifted. "You think what I've done is torture?" I nearly laughed. "Oh, sweetheart, we're just getting started. Don't tell me you've already had enough."

"Why now?" she demanded. "Why after a century of silence? Is there something else you need to use me to do? Another secret passage to take advantage of? Because I've gotta tell you, Cassius, I'm all out of useful information."

"The only thing I want from you, little killer, are your tears and blood. And eventually your death." However, her other comments were... odd. Why would I use her for information? "As to why now, you know why."

She just stared at me with resignation in her gaze. "You're not going to tell me anything, are you?"

Her statement confused me, so I said nothing.

She laughed without humor, shaking her head. "For years I've wondered if anyone even survived that night. I know deep down that they're all dead, that your master, *Dimitri*, would have made sure of it." She spoke my cousin's name with utter disdain, startling me.

Why would she hate Dimitri?

"Every day I live with the guilt of knowing I was to blame for it all," she continued. "Because I trusted you when I shouldn't have. I knew better. Yet I thought..." She trailed off, her gaze going to the table as she stole a deep breath.

I waited on pins and needles for her to continue that confession. What did she think? How did she feel about leaving me there to die? Or was that the guilt she mentioned?

And if anyone was betrayed by trust, it was me. Not her.

"You know what? It doesn't matter what I thought, does it? You're here to finish the job. That's fine. But if you win, you'll have to live with the knowledge that you only won because you disarmed me entirely by stealing my amulet. You rigged the game to make me lose before it even started. Just like you did a hundred years ago."

Wrong. I never rigged anything. I played fair. Always. However, she didn't appear to be done with her rant, so I allowed it to continue, curious as to what she'd reveal next.

Her smile was sad. "You'll never hurt me like you did then, Cassius. No matter how hard you try, I won't give you the satisfaction of destroying me all over again."

*All over again?* I repeated to myself. *What the hell is she talking about?*

She stood, planting her palms on the table and leaning forward. "So do your worst, Cassius. Play your game. Just know that nothing you can do to me now will ever compare to that night. Because that night, even with the compulsion, you had my heart. And I'll never give something so precious to you ever again."

I shot to my feet, grabbing her wrist before she could leave the room. "What compulsion?" I demanded. I had a myriad of questions plaguing my mind at her speech, but that was the one that won out among my thoughts.

"You compelled me to fall for you," she said, her tone so utterly serious I almost believed she truly felt that way.

"I never compelled you," I replied, circling the table to stand before her, my fingers still tightly wrapped around her wrist. "Why would I compel you?" Making her eat tonight didn't count. That'd been a necessary course given her stubborn response. But a hundred years ago? No. I never would have dreamed of tainting our bond with such a thing.

"You seduced me via compulsion, Cassius. It's the only explanation."

My blood raged to a smooth boil at the implication in her words. "The only explanation for what, Kseniya?"

"*Us*," she seethed, the word leaving her full lips on a quiet hiss. "I knew better than to trust you. Especially as the cousin of *King Dimitri*." She uttered his name with that subtle venom once more, her hatred for him as clear as day. "But you won, didn't you? Used me for the information and destroyed all the Romanovs. Except me."

"What information?" I asked her. "What the fuck are you talking about?" And what did she mean about me destroying all the Romanovs? She wasn't making any sense.

"Let go of me, Cassius."

"No."

"Now."

"No," I repeated. "Tell me what you mean."

"You compelled me," she said again, drawing us back to her earlier argument. "You used me, and you *compelled* me. None of it was real. Yet my heart still broke that night. Does that make you happy? Do you enjoy knowing I shattered under the realization of your betrayal?"

"I didn't compel you, Kseniya. And I don't know what you're talking about. *You* betrayed *me*. You *left*."

"Stop lying." Soft fury underlined those two words, her anger visceral and palpable. "I know what you did, Cassius. You can't change the past."

"What do you think I did?"

She just shook her head. "I won't play this game with you."

"Not everything is a game, Kseniya."

"With you, it is." She reached for her gun in the next second, her movement so quick her fingertips brushed the handle before I could catch her.

I snagged both of her wrists together in one of my palms and walked her into the wall, not bothering to be gentle or kind. She glared up at me, pain and rage bleeding through her violet eyes. I always found her beautiful before, but these new changes made her stunning, like a goddess encased in otherworldly energy. Gorgeous, really. And her ire only made her simmer that much hotter.

"You think I compelled you," I said, not a question but a statement. "I'm going to prove to you that I didn't."

She thought to turn the tables on me, to make me think for a second that perhaps she was the wronged party and not me. She'd nearly succeeded. Because for just a moment, I almost believed she didn't know the truth about what had happened. But how could that even be possible?

I knew it wasn't.

She knew exactly how it all went down.

This was just a trick. A way to taunt my heart with a flicker of hope.

Alas, no.

I saw through it now.

And her comments regarding compulsion provided me with an irresistible idea for her punishment.

"Oh, sweet, darling slayer, you're going to wish by the end of the night that you hadn't accused me of such frivolities. Because what we had was very real. Until *you* destroyed it with your actions."

She opened her mouth to speak, but I silenced her with a bruising kiss, my tongue dominant and demanding against hers. She'd said enough tonight. It was my turn to speak, to play, to shatter her in the best way possible.

"You're going to masturbate to thoughts of me all night," I told her, my compulsion strong and laced through every word. "You're going to imagine me fucking you, licking you, *tasting* you. And no matter how hard you try, you won't be able to come because it's not me."

I nipped her lower lip hard enough to bleed and smiled as

she moaned, my power taking control already, bringing her to her proverbial knees.

But I wasn't done.

"You'll exhaust yourself until you pass out, and only then will you find relief in your dreams. Except you'll dream of me fucking another woman. One who isn't you, looks nothing like you, and doesn't remind me of you at all. And you'll be so hot and bothered by it that you'll still get off and then weep at the realization that your dream is a reality."

She whimpered, her thighs clenching at the onslaught of pleasure my words were evoking. Yet pain glistened in her gaze, pain that made me smile.

"A reality because I'm going to find a willing female to fuck all night, baby. Until the sun peeks over the horizon once more, I'll be the only one you can think about while I completely forget you exist." I ran my tongue across her wound again, delighting in her shiver.

"You'll be useless to everything except your hand. It's going to hurt. You're going to cry. And if you're lucky, I'll come by tomorrow morning to lick the fresh tears from your cheeks. All the while telling you about my affair. Every sordid, explicit detail. We'll see how your heart feels after that."

I kissed the fresh drop just below her eye, loving that she was already breaking and I hadn't even left yet. I knew how her imagination worked. She'd picture it all, believe it was real because of the compulsion, and hate herself for shattering inside.

All that talk about me not being able to destroy her would fly right out the window.

Because I still affected her. I could see it in the flaring of her pupils. That wasn't compulsion. *That* was our past, peeking out at me and wondering how I could be so cruel.

I could ask her the same question.

"Have a good night, little killer," I whispered against her

mouth. "And don't even think of calling anyone over to try to help you. It won't work. The only cock that can slay you is mine." I kissed her again, more because I couldn't help myself, then shoved her away from me and gave her my coldest stare. "Sweet dreams."

I set her gun on the counter as I walked through the kitchen, then let myself out without a backward glance.

How fucking dare she belittle what we had by claiming I compelled her into it?

She deserved this fate and so much worse.

Yet as I reached the stairs, I knew I wouldn't uphold my part of the bargain. The idea of being with anyone other than her didn't appeal to me. She was the only one I wanted to make bleed. The only one I wanted to taste. The only one I wanted to *fuck*.

Which only made me hate her that much more. This spell she'd woven over me for a century had ruined my life. And now it was my turn to annihilate hers.

With a glance up at her windows from the outside, I wished her good night once more, then went for a long walk, thinking through everything she'd said.

Her curiosity about how to return to our realm was the one thing that kept percolating in my mind on repeat. It didn't make sense. She obviously knew how to go back. Yet... she'd seemed almost hopeful when I'd mentioned the ability to return.

The comments about Dimitri, or rather, her *tone*, also confused me.

Why did she hate him? He'd suffered far more than she had after it all went down. Hell, he'd lost his whole damn kingdom. It was almost as if she didn't know what really happened that night.

I ran my palm over my face, refusing to believe it.

How could she not know?

*But what if she doesn't?* another part of me thought. *What if I'm punishing her... for the wrong reasons?*

It was a possibility I had never even considered. Because it wasn't feasible. And yet, her words tonight had me walking in circles, contemplating what they really meant.

When I passed by her building much later that night, it was to find her lights still on. I almost removed the compulsion. Except then her accusation came right back, and my resolve held. She needed to understand that I never compelled her before. And after tonight, she would.

I finally returned to my residence, then punished myself as I had her—my hand working over my shaft to thoughts of her current agony, her pleasure mounting and abating, her fingers wet and sore. I wanted to replace her touch with my tongue, to lick her thoroughly while growling against her sweet little clit.

Mmm, I missed having her splayed out beneath me, writhing and hungry.

Fuck, I wanted to drill into her, bruise us both, and lose myself inside her.

But I didn't let myself go.

I halted my orgasm seconds before it began.

And went to bed with thoughts of a happier time—one where I knew love.

*My smiling Kseniya.*
*My little killer.*
*My heart.*

## CHAPTER TEN

"You look like shit," Alaric said by way of greeting.

"Thanks," I replied, too exhausted to come up with something witty to say. I'd slept like shit last night because of Cassius's fucking compulsion. And he hadn't returned in the morning like he'd suggested, which left me feeling even worse.

Because he was in bed with another woman and not thinking about me at all. Just like he'd said.

I tried and failed to not let that hurt.

Hell, it'd been a century. He wasn't celibate. *I* wasn't celibate. So what the fuck did it matter if he took another woman to bed?

But that was the problem.

It *did* matter.

And that made me hate everything about this situation even more.

He'd been right about the compulsion, something I already knew before last night. I just hadn't admitted it to myself.

It was so much easier to believe that everything between us had been a lie, that the only reason I'd ever felt anything for him was because he'd forced me to.

Last night had taken that hope and brutally squashed it

beneath the real experience of being compelled. I'd done things to myself I never would have done, crying the whole time and loathing Cassius while simultaneously missing him.

It'd been utter hell and had thoroughly driven home the point that everything I'd felt for him previously was all real.

Part of me was relieved by the revelation.

The other part of me only hated him more.

He'd proven his point on compulsion, and he'd demolished my resolve to not let him hurt my heart in the process. I'd thought it was impossible after what he'd done to me that night. However, I'd woken this morning in tears at the realization that a part of me still cared.

A part I very much wanted to eliminate.

So when Alaric called to ask if we were still on for our little "date," I'd eagerly accepted. Then he'd confirmed that the times of death for the bodies were during the fundraiser, and my heart had fractured a little more.

Because I'd been right.

This wasn't Cassius.

And if my nemesis was to be believed, then he didn't know who it was either. Which reminded me... "Do you know anything about wolves?" I asked Alaric as we waited in line outside the club.

"Wolves?" he repeated, arching a brown eyebrow. "Like the animal?"

"Shifters," I clarified.

He gave me a look, then shook his head. "Why are you asking?"

"Something Cassius said," I admitted. "Something about provoking a wolf pack."

"You spoke to Cassius?"

"Yeah. Briefly." I cleared my throat, not wanting to go into *that* little rendezvous. "He said it's not him and that he doesn't know who it is, and then mentioned a wolf pack." I held up my hand before Alaric could start. "Please don't lecture me right now. It's not like I hung out with him by choice, okay? Just... let me handle it. You and I can concentrate on this mission."

"Let you handle it," he repeated, that brow lifting even higher. "You don't seem to be handling it well at all, Vi."

I sighed. "I didn't sleep well last night." Or the night before. "But I'm fine."

He looked doubtful. Fortunately, we were next in line. "We're not done with this conversation," he warned before turning toward the bouncer and flashing his ID.

"Do you have an invitation?" the stocky male asked, his voice void of emotion.

Alaric pulled the business card from his pocket and handed it to the guy. The bald bouncer glanced at it, then nodded for us to enter, not bothering to ask for my ID.

I waited until we were inside to say, "I can't remember the last time I wasn't carded."

My purple hair and eyes gave me a young appeal. I was also somewhere around twenty-one years old, give or take a few days or months, in physical appearance.

Alaric's nod was the only indication that he'd heard me, his attention on the dark hallway stretching deep into the nightclub. Each step brought us closer to the thudding bass inside, until we met a set of stairs that led downward.

"Interesting aesthetics," I muttered, noting the sharp metal decorating the walls on the way down.

I'd worn a pair of black jeans and a black tank, something I was thankful for as we entered a room full of gothic attire. Alaric stood out in his gray shirt and jeans, his handsome face missing a handful of piercings to really fit the vibe of the room. My hair, however, suited just fine and drew several gazes.

Alaric's shoulders were stiff beside me, his discomfort showing.

I went up onto my toes and grabbed his arm for balance. My just-over-five-foot height left my lips somewhere around his collarbone, so I had to shout up at him. "Want me to pierce your nose?" I had a knife that would do the trick. Or a stake. No gun, though. I only took that on missions where I could conceal it, and a nightclub made that less than ideal.

His lips curled at the edges. "No, but thanks for the offer." He wrapped his arm around me like we were on a proper date and guided me around the bar, his gaze scanning the crowd. "Let's dance."

Dancing was the last thing I wanted to do, but it seemed to be a requirement for this rave-like scene. So I allowed him to lead me into the throng, his larger form setting a rhythm that was actually rather impressive. Especially considering he wasn't paying attention to me at all, his blue eyes glancing sharply around the room.

"What's wrong?" I asked him.

"This place doesn't feel right," he said against my ear. "I don't like it here."

"Maybe it's the underground theme?" I suggested, raising my voice just a little to be heard. But he didn't seem to be having any issues understanding me, because he shook his head.

"No, it's something else. It doesn't smell right."

I sniffed, trying to figure out what he meant. All I could scent were sweaty bodies, perfume, and a subtle whiff of cologne. I pressed my nose into Alaric's shirt, inhaling the woodsy scent. Yeah, the latter had been him. He actually smelled kind of nice.

With a shrug, I looked around, trying to find the source of his concern and coming up blank.

Then I caught a pair of reddish irises in the dark.

*Vampire.*

It was a subtle glow that I wasn't sure anyone else could see, but my slayer traits allowed me to pick up on it as a warning sign.

Three more appeared in my peripheral vision.

"Ric," I whispered. "There are at least four suckers in the club." *Suckers* was a term I used in place of *vampires* to avoid anyone overhearing me. Including the leeches waiting in the dark.

"More," Alaric replied, his movements changing just a hair from fluid to cautious. "At least twelve."

"*Twelve?*" I repeated, blinking. That qualified as a nest. And if one existed in this nightclub, then we were in for a world of trouble.

Just as I thought it, I heard the change in the beat. The subtle shift of doors, closing us in on the sides.

We'd just walked into a feeding den.

A blood rave.

A fucking nightmare.

All because of the card Alaric had found in the pocket of that victim.

*Cassius*, I realized. *He did this.*

He'd set up a trap with the intent of watching me fail. A mortal slayer, against an army of undead.

It was just the kind of climax he'd enjoy.

"We need to get out of here," I said urgently.

But Alaric shook his head. "It's too late, Vi. The party has already started."

The lights went out on his final word.

The music grew in volume.

And then the screaming started.

"Fuck!" I ducked as a net fell from the ceiling. Alaric hit the ground beside me, his curse lost to the shrieks of chaos whirling around us. Humans began to trample, squirming to get away from the netting.

Something sticky touched my face, making me flinch. *Is that…blood? Oh my God.* The material above wasn't mesh but metal. *Sharp* metal.

Alaric grabbed me suddenly, rolling us out of the way of a stampede. "Keep your shoulder against mine and crawl!" he shouted, leading the way. I wasn't sure how he could see or where he was leading us, but I followed him anyway.

People tripped over us, kicked my thigh, my side, and one even hit my head, but I didn't let it stop me. I'd trained with Alaric long enough to know he would have my back when it counted, and he didn't disappoint me now. He stopped when we reached a wall, his hand landing on my thigh as he pulled me close.

"The front entrance is chained off." He spoke the words right against my ear. "But there's a back door being guarded by two big vamps. I can't sense what's beyond it, though."

"How can you even see?" I demanded, completely blind to the darkness and nearly deaf to the insanity unleashing through the air. Between the thudding bass and screaming patrons, I felt nearly paralyzed by my senses.

Alaric stiffened beside me, then jumped to his feet. I tried to follow, only to have my sight blinded by the lights suddenly coming on.

I stumbled to the side, my world spinning as the stench of pennies hit my nose. I sneezed on impulse, my stake already in my hand.

My vision began to clear, the reddish hue painting the room in a ghastly glow that illuminated the death scene sprawling throughout the dance floor.

Not everyone was dead.

Actually, most were alive.

But it was a horde of scraped limbs, tangled torsos, and frightened humans. They were pushing toward the exit, trying to get through the chains, while the vampires stood around laughing.

It was a mob mentality gone wrong, the crowd seeking an escape and not caring whom they trampled on to get there.

Some were standing along the walls like me and Alaric. Others weren't moving on the floor. It all reminded me of a macabre rave, with the techno still blaring, the lights sparkling in red flashes of light, and the heavy nets reminiscent of a hunting trap.

We had to do something. We had to stop this.

But this was unlike anything I'd ever seen.

Vampires lived in secret, and there was nothing "secret" about this. There had to be at least fifty humans down here. Did they intend to kill them? Well, they'd have to, or the media would catch wind of this massacre.

Unless... was that the point?

Had Cassius sent me here so I could see the nightlife scene that was unfolding within the vampire underworld?

Something had shifted. A new hierarchy rising to the surface. Was it him? Did he intend to rule New York City the way his cousin ruled the Vampire Dynasty? Was this what the world had turned into without the slayers keeping the bloodsuckers in line?

My heart skipped a beat.

The vampires back home were essentially gods, making it entirely possible that they'd dominated the world. There were other supernaturals there, too. Wolves. Witches. Fae.

I swallowed, picturing how easy it would have been for them to enslave humans and create something as brutal as this scene before me.

Only, I wasn't in that realm anymore.

I was in a realm where vampires died with a fluid *pop*.

A stake through the heart and they crumbled into ash.

Cassius could try to influence the supernaturals of this

world, but it wouldn't work. Because E.V.I.E. would slay them all.

Starting tonight.

I rolled my shoulders, taking in the scene again with a renewed priority. No more pity parties. No more worries. If Cassius wanted to watch me suffer, then I'd give him one hell of a show.

I twirled my stake in my hand and looked at Alaric. "Let's get to work."

His lips pulled back in a feral grin. "You go left. I'll go right."

"See you on the other side," I agreed, hoping like hell the red light remained. If it didn't, well, then I'd have to get creative.

Because no way in hell was I going to die tonight.

*All right, Cassius. You want to play? Let's play.*

# CASSIUS

## CHAPTER ELEVEN

SAPPHIRE DREW her nail along the tanzanite stone, her lips curling downward. "Who created this?"

"Roskana," I replied, checking my watch for the thousandth time. I'd hoped to be back in the other realm by now, but it'd taken me a while to track down Dimitri's pet witch.

The petite, blue-haired female had pledged her allegiance to my cousin and his cause about a decade ago, vowing to help him retrieve his throne. I suspected there was something she wanted in return, but she hadn't voiced it yet.

"Her magic is very different from mine," Sapphire mused, allowing the amulet to play over her fingers. "My incantations won't work on it."

"Meaning you can't use it to traverse realms?" I asked her, needing clarification. It dawned on me when I woke up this morning that I had a way to test Kseniya's comments from last night—by giving her amulet to Sapphire for her evaluation.

"I suspect it holds the power, but it doesn't feel obvious to me. Roskana didn't make this with the intent to travel. It's meant to protect. Which means it could have manifested the escape purely as a result of helping the owner survive." She shrugged, handing it back to me. "You would have to ask her if it can be used to travel back, but I suspect she might not know."

"Why do you suspect that?"

"Because this one has never been used for that purpose. I'd be able to sense it otherwise." Sapphire had a knack for sensing the history of an object, something not all witches could do.

"You're saying Kseniya has never traveled realms with this amulet?"

"Correct. She's only used that necklace for her immortality. There's also an anti-compulsion charm on it that appears to have been added after she left our reality. She's never had to use it, though, so I'm not sure why it's there." She shrugged again. "Another question for Roskana."

I frowned. *Yeah, another question. Of which I had about a thousand now.*

Because this implied Kseniya's curiosity had been real. Which suggested that everything else she'd told me... I swallowed, unable to complete that thought.

Instead, I focused on Sapphire. "Thank you. I'm going to go check in with Dimitri." Which would only prolong my return, but I needed his opinion.

"Tell him I'm close to locating Anastasia," Sapphire said softly, returning to the papers sprawled out across a long glass table. "Maybe another week or two." She sounded almost lost to her words, her blue eyes taking on a faraway gleam as she returned to her task of dismantling wards and searching through space and time.

Dimitri would be relieved to learn how close his witch was to finally locating the slayer. She was vital to our plans and perhaps the only one who could help us successfully remove Grigori from the reformed Vampire Dynasty throne.

I uttered a soft goodbye to the witch, but she was too lost

in her thoughts to hear me. At least she'd been able to pay attention long enough to give me the answer I needed.

Tucking the amulet into my pants pocket, I headed out to find my cousin.

He wasn't far, his residence on the coast of Greece not nearly as vast as his former home. All the white walls and splashes of blue were appropriate for the region but were missing the golds and opulence of home.

I missed Russia.

But I didn't miss what it had become in our absence. Grigori ruled the dynasty with a penchant for gluttonous behavior and debauchery. Humans were food. Slayers were toys. And vampires were expected to follow a strict hierarchical regimen, worshipping him at the top while vying for a lieutenant role at his side.

The fools would never replace Roman. He was too valuable to Grigori. But I suspected Grigori enjoyed the constant challenges leveled at his second-in-command. They all ensured Roman remained in his position as Grigori's right-hand man.

Which was precisely why we needed Anastasia Romanov.

Dimitri stood on the black sand beach, watching the sun set over the horizon.

"Did you find what you were looking for?" he asked as I approached him from behind, his gaze on the water beyond. He had his hands tucked into his black pants, his shirt a similar shade that matched his dark head of hair. We were opposites in that way—my own strands a stark white to his sable shade.

No one would know we were related by looking at us. While our statures were similar in height and athleticism, his skin was tan, whereas I was pale, and his eyes resembled the ocean, while mine shone with a silver gleam against the dimming light.

He turned as I stopped beside him, his expression contemplative. "Well?"

"Sapphire says she should have Anastasia's location in a week or two."

"Then I hope your revenge is going as planned," he drawled. "Because I'm going to need you soon."

I pulled the amulet from my pocket, allowing the sun to play off the pretty tanzanite stone. "Sapphire confirmed this has never been used to travel realms."

"Meaning your Kseniya hasn't used it to come back."

I nodded, thoughtful. "It's possible Roskana has teleported them."

"Your tone tells me you don't believe that."

I didn't. One thing I never understood was how they could have left Anastasia to her fate. Kseniya had always loved that woman like a sister. But I'd spent so long thinking everything she'd ever proclaimed was a lie that I'd ignored the obvious. "They haven't tried to save Anastasia because they don't know how to."

"An interesting theory," Dimitri agreed. "Have you tried asking Kseniya?"

"I've been a little busy torturing her."

He smiled. "I bet. Leaving her mortal and alone is a punishment in itself. She must be losing her shit over the missing necklace."

I thought about that. "Actually, other than demanding it back a few times, she's not been all that bothered. She was more interested in learning how I found her. And she seems to hate you."

His eyebrows lifted. "Because I'm a vampire?"

"She called you *King Dimitri*. Then claimed we'd won. But I have no idea what she thinks we won, or if it was all just a lie meant to confuse me more."

"What would she gain by crafting such a tale?" Dimitri

asked, his blue eyes swirling with the power of his bloodline. "Why waste your time?"

"Perhaps to convince me not to kill her," I said, the words making me frown to utter such a frivolity out loud. The Kseniya I knew would never play that hand in a game. "I spent the last century analyzing the woman and her choices. I was so certain I had her all figured out. And now I find out her amulet has never been used to travel realms."

It left me wondering what else I'd misjudged.

"She said she accidentally portaled to the new realm." I was thinking out loud, recalling everything she'd claimed last night. "She also accused me of using her for information."

"What information?"

"About the secret tunnels."

"Beneath Romanov Palace?"

"I think so," I replied, considering our conversation and everything else she'd revealed. "She said I destroyed the Romanovs."

Dimitri grunted. "She can thank Grigori for that."

"What if she doesn't know?" I asked him. "What if she...?" I trailed off, thinking it through. "If she thinks I betrayed the knowledge of the tunnels to you, and that you destroyed the Romanovs as King..."

"That would paint you as the villain of her story," Dimitri surmised. "Or she's fucking with you, just like she did a century ago."

"But what was her motive?" It was the one question I never could answer. "Why leave me for Grigori to find?"

If what she said about portaling was true—that she'd accidentally jumped realms—then that would mean she hadn't abandoned me at all. That she'd fled to escape potential death. And if she didn't know how to return, that would explain why she'd left me to rot in that cell.

"What if she had no idea that Grigori had captured me?"

That would demolish all of my assumptions about her. Every scenario I crafted was based on her setting me up for eventual incarceration. "He told me she bargained my life for her own."

I hadn't believed him at first, but when she never came for me, the truth of it settled inside me, brewing a deep-seated hatred founded in betrayal.

She'd sentenced me to hell.

Unless…

"Grigori has a penchant for using matters of the heart against his victims," Dimitri murmured, his oceanic irises whirling once more. "It's entirely possible that he crafted a tale meant to poison you against your own soul. He'd see it as the ultimate way to weaken a man. And if you killed Kseniya as a result—"

"I'd never forgive myself," I realized with a start.

Shit, I'd have a hell of time forgiving myself for all the things I'd already done.

"I need to talk to her," I said, my thumb already resting over the ring on my right index finger. "You know how to reach me if anything develops in the interim."

"Cassius." Dimitri's tone stopped me from portal-jumping. "A suggestion."

"Yes?"

"Bring her back for a visit." He looked at me. "Her reaction should provide you with all the answers you seek."

I studied him for a moment, then nodded. "You're right. If she believes you killed her family, she won't be able to hide her rage."

"And if you tell her what we know about Anastasia's current fate, you'll be able to read the emotion of that reveal. Not even an award-winning actress could fake that sort of pain. Not to our senses."

He was right.

The Kseniya I knew—the woman I'd fallen in love with —would be ripped apart by the knowledge of what had happened to her former friend.

If Kseniya was the female I once adored, she'd react violently. And if she was the vixen I'd created in my mind, then she'd try to feign a reaction—a reaction I would see right through.

"I'm going to get her."

"Good." Dimitri glanced up at the darkening sky. "Perhaps we can convince her to help our cause."

"Something tells me that's going to be hard to do."

His lips twitched. "You'll figure it out. You're resourceful like that." His eyes found mine once more, his expression void of emotion. "Just remember that she can't know the full truth about what we have planned."

I nodded, understanding.

There was only one way to defeat Grigori.

And it wasn't without significant cost.

"You know where my loyalty lies, cousin," I told him.

"I do," he agreed. "I also know who owns your heart."

"Owned," I corrected.

"Sure. Go find your slayer. You know where to find me." He turned then, heading back up the beach to his home. His shoulders were tight, the weight of all our futures hanging upon them with such force that it was a wonder he remained standing. But if anyone could handle the pressure, it was him.

Pressing my thumb to the ruby on my ring, I whispered the incantation Sapphire had taught me, and navigated my way through the portal realms.

Rather than go to my place in New York City, I let myself out of the network in an alley near Kseniya's building and jogged up the stairs to her flat. Knocking twice, I waited. A whine from the other side of the door had my lips curling downward. Using the ring, I created a quick portal that allowed me to step through the locked entrance and found Luci pacing on the other side.

"What's wrong?" I asked her, immediately sensing the distress in her expression.

She snapped at me and gestured to the door with her nose, then made an impatient noise.

"Do you need to go out?" I wondered out loud, uncertain of how often a hellhound required use of the outdoor facilities.

She growled, then shook out her black coat as though negating my guess.

"Is it Kseniya?" It was a natural second theory, considering Luci's clear affinity for my little killer.

Her low whine had my heart skipping a beat.

"She's in trouble," I translated, understanding the antsy behavior now. "Do you know where she is?"

Luci huffed as though to say, *Obviously*.

And she couldn't get out because she lacked the ability to unlock and open doors. Right.

"Where's your collar and leash?"

She growled.

"I can't just walk you through Manhattan without one," I said, exasperated.

She darted into the other room and returned with the items in her mouth, spitting them out at my feet. Then I swore she lifted an expectant brow, saying something along the lines of, *Hurry the hell up*.

I wrapped the leather around her neck and hooked on her leash. She was at the door a second later, her nose pressed against the wood.

Using my ring, I created another portal and took us to the alley below again. "Lead the way," I told her.

# VIOLET

## CHAPTER TWELVE

I ROLLED MY SHOULDERS, my body tight with exhaustion and the blossoming bruises created by the frenzied humans. But I wasn't about to let a little pain get me down.

It was time to dance.

I had my lucky stake, precision, and a lifetime of training on my side. These bloodsuckers didn't stand a chance.

*I hope you're watching, Cassius,* I thought, shifting from foot to foot, preparing to dance. *You're next.*

The beat of the club seemed to shift as I engaged my lethal side, the slayer in me coming out to play with a ferocity I kept well hidden. Cassius thought I'd grown complacent in my old age? Well, the joke was on him. I'd stayed at the top of my game, preparing for a moment just like this.

Ignoring the fatigue in my limbs, I strode forward, locating a few vampires on my side, and went to work. The first one went down with a surprised *pop*, his body bursting into flames and instantly turning to ash. Humans shrieked around me, their shock a palpable wave that only seemed to excite the thirst in the room.

At least until the vampires realized what was coming for them.

I had two more in my sight, their chests blinking in the

red light. *Metal*, I realized, calculating where and how to hit them. They had the chains pulled tight across their pecs, wearing it like old-fashioned armor but in a gothic setting. Bizarre, yet oddly appropriate for this nightclub.

And really damn frustrating because it blocked my target —their hearts.

Even more frustrating was that they'd noticed my approach thanks to their friend's fiery demise.

I fell into a crouch as they prowled forward, their gazes sharp and narrowing in on the stake in my hand.

The big vamp on the left lifted his lips into a snarl, while his shorter, bald buddy just licked his lips. I smiled. "You hungry?" I asked him, twirling my stake. "Come and get me."

He grinned, accepting my invitation. My blood thrummed with excitement, the slayer in me thirsting for death. I measured their pace, anticipating their arrival, only to suddenly be yanked backward by my hair.

A growling beast stared down at me, his eyes red and terrifying, his jaws snapping cruelly toward my neck.

*What the fuck?*

This wasn't a vampire, yet I sensed the afterlife lurking inside him. It didn't make any sense.

I struggled against him, trying to find my footing, when a blinding light flared through the room, the UV bomb one Alaric must have had in his pocket. The creature holding me shrieked, releasing me to bound back into the shadows, his skin on fire yet not bursting into ash. The two vampires I'd originally intended to play with went up in flames, sizzling to crispy remains on the floor. But not the thing that had grabbed me.

"We need to get the fuck out of here!" Alaric shouted at me, his hulking form somehow appearing at my side.

"What the hell is that thing?"

"Not a vampire."

"No shit." I watched it spin and howl and set everything around it on fire. Clothing and upholstery were all blazing to life, igniting the sprinkler system overhead. Humans were crying, the nightclub clouded in chaos and smoke and a streaming rain. It all happened in the span of seconds.

More vampires poured into the room, the entire underground unleashing into the insanity.

*Trapdoors*, I realized. Had they all been waiting for their feast?

Blood sprayed, a true massacre unfolding around us.

One of the leeches lunged at me, and I struck upward with my stake, nailing him right in the heart before turning to face another.

Alaric was at my back, fighting for his life as I tore through the army descending upon us.

This was not survivable.

A trap meant to take down even the best E.V.I.E. had to offer, right in the middle of fucking Brooklyn.

*How?* I marveled, my head spinning as I tried to piece it all together, my body moving on autopilot.

Then that monster turned toward me again, his skin blackened with soot, his red eyes gleaming with rage. He had grown to twice a normal man's size, his fingers shaped into talons.

*A shifter.*

Cassius's comments regarding wolf packs came back to me in a flash. Was this what he meant? Had we stepped into some sort of conflict between the vampires and the wolves?

But that thing was more than just a shifter.

He had *fangs*.

I watched as he bent to rip out the throat of a pale-skinned female, his tongue snaking around her neck and lapping greedily at her essence. All the while, he watched me, his gaze holding a promise of death. *My* death.

A hand caught my arm, Alaric's voice in my ear. "Let's go!"

But I couldn't move.

I was captivated and enthralled by the beast stalking toward me.

All the others seemed to bow to him, his presence holding a command they clearly revered.

Then another UV bomb went off, drawing me out of the moment and back to Alaric as he dragged me toward the exit.

Someone had cut through the chains, allowing the humans to rush up the stairs.

But a door held them all captive at the end.

My head spun, escape seeming impossible.

The music reached a higher pitch, the beat thundering through my skull. Alaric crumpled beside me, his hands on his ears. I thought he yelled a word, but I didn't catch it, my nose twitching at an almond-like scent infiltrating the room.

*What now?*

I blinked, my vision clouding. My knees buckled, sending me to the floor beside Alaric.

Victory sounded in the distance.

Howls.

Or were they growls?

Everything around me spun, the mortals all seeming to grow quiet as one while my enhanced senses hung on. My slayer bloodline strengthened every part of me, making me less human, but it was my amulet that ensured my immortality. Without it, I could die.

No, I *would* die.

Because the vampires were surrounding us now, their expressions triumphant, and my limbs refused to move. I was trapped motionless on the dirty concrete, watching my fate walk toward me with a mouth of too-sharp teeth. The lights were all on now. The creature had returned to a normal size, his red eyes shifting to dark brown orbs.

"Get them all in the cages," he demanded. "Except that one. She's mine. Actually, tie up her partner, too. I want to make him watch this time."

*This time?* I thought, my brow furrowing. Or, well, my brow attempted to, anyway. I couldn't exactly move.

I was also no longer able to see.

But I could hear just fine. I could also *feel*.

The world seemed to shift around me, cold fingers touching parts of my body they had no business caressing.

My clothes whispered across my skin, leaving me naked on a metal chair. I slouched forward, but a leather belt around my middle held me upright. Then they clasped something solid around my ankles and wrists.

Everything danced by in a blur.

Time became meaningless.

I just waited for my body to catch up with my still-alert mind.

This was the downside to my unique bloodline. The humans were all blissfully unaware, while I remained just lucid enough to know what was happening to me. I supposed it gave me an advantage in the sense that I wouldn't lose my shit when I finally came to again. I already knew they'd put me in a room of sorts, perhaps a cell. The door had sounded heavy, closing with a decisive thud. Chains clanked to my right, the echo of metal snapping into place.

*Alaric.* I could smell his woodsy aftershave.

He was going to be pissed when he woke up.

But what had the creature meant by "this time"?

Voices rose, their words indecipherable. A horde of shouts soon followed. I tried to frown, still a prisoner inside my mind.

Doors opened and closed.

Curses followed.

Was that an apology from someone?

*What's happening now?*

The air seemed to shift, power infiltrating the atmosphere and raising the hairs along my arms. I recognized that electrical current and the man who came with it.

*Cassius.*

I wanted to growl.

He must be so pleased with the trap he'd set. However, two against fifty was hardly fair, especially when humans were in the way and creating greater concerns.

I also hadn't anticipated facing a beast. It was sort of cheating on his part, while also serving as a fault on mine. Because I should have known by now to always prepare for the unexpected.

My fingers began to tingle, the effects of the drug beginning to wane. *Finally.*

Unfortunately, it was just in time for Cassius to arrive. He'd quickly subdue me in this state, particularly as my hands were cuffed behind my back.

Hell, he'd subdue me in almost every state.

That had turned me on once upon a time.

Not today.

A snarl startled me out of my misery, the sound familiar and coming from my Luci. *What is she doing here?*

My heart thumped in my chest.

Had Cassius brought her here? Did he intend to hurt her? *No!*

If he touched a hair on her head, I would—

A lick to my shin made everything inside me still. Then a pair of paws found my thighs as Luci used me as a stepping stool to bring her nose to mine with another lick. "*Ruff*," she woofed softly, shocking the hell out of me.

She *never* barked. And certainly not like that.

"She's okay," Cassius assured her, his presence taunting me into awareness. His cologne drifted across my senses, his fingers dancing along my neck.

Luci huffed as though to agree, then backed off my legs.

"I need the keys," he said, his touch leaving my neck.

My hellhound gave another puff of air, her nails clacking over the concrete as she scampered around. A groan from nearby sounded, then a yowl of pain. I mentally flinched, but the sound hadn't come from my baby. It'd come from something else.

"You taking that back with us?" Cassius asked conversationally.

*Taking what back?* I wanted to ask him. *And what the hell are you talking about?*

Luci gave a low growl, causing Cassius to chuckle. "That's fine."

*Is he talking to her?* I wondered, my eyelids refusing to lift.

Cassius's fingertips brushed my arm as he went to my wrists. The hairs along my skin danced in the wake of his touch, my blood heating on impulse. "Your mind is aware right now, isn't it, sweet slayer?" he whispered against my ear, his body behind mine. "That's why Luci licked you. She knows you can sense her."

The hellhound in question snorted as though to say, *Obviously.*

"Your connection to her is unique and rather beautiful," he marveled. "She led me straight to you."

*Led you to me?* I wanted to ask, not following his statement. *You set this trap. How could she lead you anywhere?*

"What the fuck are you doing?" a deep voice demanded.

"Taking what's mine," Cassius replied, my wrists falling free from the restraints.

"Yours?"

"Yes." The lethal edge in that single-worded reply had my heart skipping a beat. Cassius rarely used that tone. It was a warning in itself, one the other male clearly didn't hear.

"Jed isn't going to be pleased. He said to put her and the wolf here and guard them until he returned."

"Consider yourself relieved of guard duty," Cassius returned.

"That's not how this works."

Cassius sighed, his hands settling on my shoulders. "Luci, would you care to do the honors, or shall I?"

She gave a little snort, then snarled, and a shriek followed as heat warmed the room.

"Such a useful companion," Cassius praised, his touch drifting to my leg and down to my ankle as he moved to my side. The restraints holding my feet in place disappeared, his hand massaging the area as though to stimulate warmth.

The distinct noise of bone crunching met my ears, telling me Luci had turned the vampire into her own personal chew toy. He wouldn't die from her munching, but he would be in a hell of a lot of pain.

Something cold touched my side—a knife slicing through the leather restraint. Cassius caught me before my body could slip sideways, then carefully scooped me up into his arms. His chest cushioned my head as my mind fought to catch up with what he was doing.

If this had all been his trap, then why was he releasing me?

"Right, then. Shall we, Luci?" he asked.

She growled.

"What now?"

She snuffed, conveying something to him.

"Him? Seriously?"

The little whine that followed was her version of a "Yes."

Cassius grumbled under his breath and set me down again on the hard slab. "Fine. But only because it'll place him in my debt."

Luci grunted and went back to her bone-crunching.

My whole body shivered against the cold ground, my limbs slowly awakening. I needed my body to move faster, for the toxin suffocating my senses to lift, but it was all a thick haze that left me useless on the ground.

I *hated* feeling weak, a fact Cassius knew.

Was this all a ploy to use it against me? To play with me? To hurt me? To make me feel even worse about failing this little game?

A low growl reverberated through the air, one that didn't belong to Luci. "Don't fucking touch me," Alaric snapped, his voice alert and deep and filled with fury.

"Trust me, if I could avoid it, I would. Now stop slobbering all over yourself and let me finish."

"I can save myself."

"Sure. All that silver would be really easy for you to remove."

"Fuck you," Alaric seethed. Metal squeaked in protest of being twisted the wrong way, resulting in Cassius sighing in annoyance.

"I wouldn't try it, wolf. The drugs are still working their way out of your system, and a sparring match with me will only result in your definite death. Which apparently would upset Luci, and by proxy, my Kseniya. Both are consequences I would like to avoid."

*Wolf?* I thought to myself. *Alaric is a wolf?*

Jude's words came back to me regarding Alaric and how I hadn't paid much attention to his hints. Now it all came together in a flash—the way he'd scented the dead bodies from the street yesterday, how he'd been able to see in the dark, even his woodsy aftershave... *He's a shifter.*

So what had the creature meant about making him watch again?

It seemed I wasn't the only one hiding things from my partner.

"Touch her and I'll kill you," Alaric warned.

Cassius laughed. "Oh, I'm going to do a lot more than touch her, wolf. You can count on it."

I shivered at the insinuation in his tone, bewilderment running through me at a rapid pace. None of this made sense. The wolf thing, yeah, okay, that did. But Cassius's present actions were lost on me.

Had he set this up or not?

And if he had, why free me? Why help Alaric?

"I'm leaving that last one for you to break," Cassius said. "A few twists ought to do the trick. When you're done, head out and go left, then up. And try to be fast about it. The distraction I left for Jed and his followers is going to end in about thirty minutes."

My world moved again as Cassius lifted me from the ground.

"Oh, and next time, be more forthcoming. I know you could smell the hybrid and his pals before you entered. Which means you walked my Kseniya right into the proverbial wolf's den, all the while knowing the risk. I understand and respect your motives, but if you ever put her life in jeopardy like that again, I'll kill you myself."

Cassius snapped his fingers and whistled. "Time to go, Luci."

She grunted at him.

"Then bring the arm. Just don't get that shit on my furniture."

My brow furrowed—providing me with momentary relief because I'd actually moved—but my lips refused to work. I wanted to ask what he meant by *his* furniture. However, I suspected I'd have an answer in a few minutes.

"Remember, twist, then go left and up. Good luck, wolf."

# CASSIUS

## CHAPTER THIRTEEN

*FUCK.*

*Fuck.*

*Fuck.*

The word rolled through my head on repeat as I cradled Kseniya's curvy little body against my chest.

When I'd arrived at the nightclub to find the massacre of blood and human remains, my heart had fucking stopped. Then Luci had grabbed my hand with her mouth and tugged me not so gently toward a door at the back. Down we'd ventured into the dungeons of this world's version of hell.

Several vampires had stood near the bottom, guarding the door. I'd destroyed them all in a matter of seconds, leaving a scowling hellhound at my side. I hadn't understood her annoyance until I saw her handle that idiot who tried to stop me from freeing Kseniya.

Apparently, Luci had a thing for vampire bones. When I'd killed all the guards, they'd turned to ash, leaving her without a treat. Now she had a humerus in her mouth that continued to regenerate while she chewed. That had to hurt the owner like hell, but I didn't care. He deserved the torment for getting in my way.

As did the one they called *Jed*. I didn't know him, but I intended to meet him after observing the aftermath of his nightclub bloodbath. However, there'd been more pressing matters on my mind tonight—namely, finding Kseniya and freeing her from that hellhole.

Now that I had her secured in my arms, I felt a little better, but that damn curse continued to riot in my thoughts.

Without her amulet, she could be killed.

Something I'd thought to use as a taunt against her, yet it'd backfired completely. Because someone else had almost taken her from me.

A hybrid, from the smell of him.

No wonder he created such a mess. Wolves weren't known for their table manners. But to take out a nightclub would raise a lot of red flags. If the slayers didn't take him out, other vampires would because he was putting their very existence at risk.

Although, he seemed to have an army of trained minions.

I shook my head. *Not my realm, not my responsibility.*

Hmm, but my little killer would probably consider it her task to dismantle his power trip and destroy him. Maybe I'd help her, after we had a long talk about the past.

She began to stir against me, her eyelids lifting to reveal a pair of beautiful purple irises. It really was a striking color on her, making her all the more alluring. Or perhaps that was just her. I'd always found her irresistible. Now was no different.

"Why?" she rasped, her voice rough and barely audible.

"Why what, sweetheart?" I asked as I set her on the marble counter between the two sinks in my bathroom. I gently guided her back to rest against the mirror, not wanting her to fall over and gain yet another bruise. She was already bloodied up enough, something that should have thrilled me but didn't.

Talking to Sapphire, and then to Dimitri, had fucked everything up in my head. I no longer knew what to believe where Kseniya was concerned. However, I intended to get to the bottom of it, just as soon as I cleaned her up a bit.

"Are you asking why I saved you?" I guessed when she didn't elaborate.

She stared at me for a long moment, her body still not fully recovered from whatever sleep agent Jed had used in the nightclub. Given the general disarray of the scene, I suspected he'd played with his food a little first, allowing them to run around in terror before knocking them out cold. There'd also been metal wires everywhere, suggesting a net had been used as well.

Sick bastard.

Kseniya cleared her throat, then dipped her head slowly in the affirmative.

"Because the only one allowed to hurt you, sweet slayer, is me," I said, bending to brush my lips over hers. "Now I'm going to clean you up, and we're going to have a chat."

She responded by slowly lifting her middle finger.

I smirked. "Careful, baby. I might take that as an invitation."

"It's not." Her voice came out a little stronger, but she grimaced as though it pained her to speak. I didn't like that.

"Did they injure you?" I asked, running my palms over her nude form, checking for any significant damage.

Bruises blemished her pale skin, and she had a few cuts that I suspected came from the wires, but she otherwise appeared all right on the surface. Though, that didn't mean she lacked internal damage.

I brought my wrist to my mouth and bit deep. "Here." I lifted the wound to her lips. "Drink."

She glared at me. "No."

"It'll help you heal faster," I pointed out. "It'll also give you the energy you need to release yourself from whatever drug he used on you. Be smart, not stubborn."

Her eyes narrowed more, but I could see the wheels turning inside her head. Accepting my strength would provide her with the energy her body desperately craved. It would also allow her an escape from the weakness she had to be feeling at present.

And if there was one thing I knew about Kseniya, it was her hatred for frailty.

Her mouth sealed around my wrist, her tongue working over the laceration to lap up the essence her wounded form badly needed. My cock hardened in response, the intimacy of the moment one neither of us could deny. I saw her interest in the dilation of her pupils and the flaring of her nostrils. Her thighs clenched next, her sweet arousal an enchantment in the air that caused my stomach to tighten with need.

She was the only one I ever allowed to drink from me.

The only one I ever cared enough about to heal.

An entire history existed between us, one underlined in illicit lust and forbidden touches such as this. They all came to the forefront of my thoughts, dragging me closer to her.

I'd nearly lost her tonight. Because I'd left her inferior and alone. Because she'd fallen into a madman's trap. Because she'd been too exhausted to see the danger lurking right before her eyes.

I could see that exhaustion in her now, in the heavy bags beneath her eyes, the way her limbs seemed thinner and more frail than usual.

She hadn't slept last night because of my compulsion, then she'd walked into that club without her amulet, her duty to her job outweighing her own will to survive.

I shook my head, frustrated with both her and myself. When I came here for her, I intended to play and torment her, but finding her battered and bruised in that chair hadn't pleased me at all. And something told me that even if I'd been the one to reduce her to that state, I still wouldn't have enjoyed it.

She took one final swallow, then removed her mouth, her eyelashes fanning over her cheeks as she lowered her gaze in astute submission. I didn't like it. I didn't like belittling my darling killer in such a way. I wanted her strong and formidable, not sad and broken.

Fuck, it was such a conundrum.

A week ago, I wanted to watch her burn.

And now... now that I had her naked before me, meek and humbled, I wanted nothing more than to watch her rise from the ashes and blossom into the fiery phoenix I knew existed beneath her soft skin.

I cupped her jaw, tilting her head backward, forcing her violet eyes to meet mine. Then I reached into my pocket to pull out her amulet with my opposite hand and pressed it to her palm. "Put it back on," I told her. "I won't take it again."

Unless I intended to kill her. That would be the only exception. And if I found out all of this had been a lie, that she was truly just a masterful performer, then I would annihilate her.

However, for now, I wanted her strong. I wanted my Kseniya back. I wanted my equal, my partner, my love.

With shaking hands, she fastened the chain around her neck and shivered as the magic reacted to her wounds, helping her to heal in time with my blood, restoring the slayer inside her.

I stepped away from her to focus on the shower, the two heads in the ceiling springing to life to drench the obsidian rocks below them.

My entire bathroom had been crafted from a variety of dark colors, the ornate counters composed of black marble and adorned in gold fixtures. The floor was a slate gray, and the walls were an almost silver tone. I preferred darkness; it called to my soul. Which was why my adjoining bedroom held a similar color palette.

Kseniya's cheeks were flushed as I returned, her muscles twitching to life as though preparing for a fight. But the urge left her as I began unbuttoning my shirt, allowing the fabric to part and reveal my toned physique beneath.

Vampires in my world were forever frozen at the age of their turning, but our bodies could occasionally fluctuate. Not by much. However, nine decades in a prison with nothing to do other than work out and keep up my strength had crafted me into a slab of defined muscle. Her purple irises ran over me with appreciation, her lips parting as my shirt fell unceremoniously to the ground at my feet.

I removed my shoes next. Then my socks and pants. And it wasn't until I had my hands on my black boxers that her mind seemed to catch up.

"What are you doing?" Her voice was much clearer now, the tone healthy and right.

"Taking a shower with you."

"Why?"

"Because I want to." I also needed to reassure myself that she could stand without hurting herself. A ridiculous notion because I knew she could now that she'd rejuvenated her spirits with the amulet and my blood. But that didn't stop me from removing my boxer shorts and moving to stand naked before her.

Her eyes fell to my groin, her breath coming out in a shudder. "Cassius…"

I ignored the warning in her tone and lifted her off the counter. Her feet touched the floor, her legs giving a slight wobble. She clutched my arms, wincing at the display of instability.

"It's okay, Kseniya," I whispered. "You'll be yourself again very soon. Then we can spar if you want, but I'm washing your hair first." It'd been so long since I felt those silky strands between my fingers. Too long since I'd really *touched* her.

My throat worked over a swallow, my entire body primed and ready for her and not at all caring that our circumstances were still in shambles.

This woman was mine, had always been mine, would always be *mine*.

Which was why I'd have to kill her if everything Grigori had told me turned out to be true. It would be the only way for me to dismantle this spell she held over me.

I pressed my lips to hers, hungry for a taste, and found her mouth just as eager as mine. Her grip on my biceps tightened, her body arching toward me rather than away from me. I pulled her closer, then walked us both toward the waiting shower without breaking our kiss. Her steps weren't perfect, her strength not yet fully restored, but she pushed through it with the heart of a warrior.

Water rained down around us, bathing us in warmth as I reached around her to close the glass door. Then I enveloped her in my arms, my tongue seeking hers. She practically melted against me, our history a thriving heartbeat between us.

The hatred I should feel for her seemed to slip through the drain at our feet. Maybe because of the truth Sapphire had revealed, or perhaps it was a result of just missing my other half.

*Fuck.*

I ripped off the band holding up her hair and threaded my fingers through the thick strands, needing to embrace her. She clutched me just as harshly, her nails digging into my arms and drawing blood in the process. It had always been like this between us, passionate and violent and so utterly mind-blowing.

But before I could take it to the next level and completely destroy her with my mouth, she yanked away from me, panting, her eyes flashing. "I don't understand."

"That makes two of us," I admitted, breathing almost as heavily as her, my chest heaving with the need to drag her back into me and fuck her against the wall.

"You left that card for me to find. Then you set the trap in the club. Now..." She paused to steal a huge gulp of air. "Now you're kissing me? Saving me? Healing me?" She shook her head, her expression one of acute bewilderment. "*Why?*"

"What card?" I asked. "And I didn't set a trap, Kseniya."

"The card on the dead body in the deli."

"You think I staged that scene?"

"Didn't you?" she countered. "Isn't this all just one of your infamous games?"

I nearly laughed. "Infamous games?"

"Stop playing with me, Cassius."

"Never," I retorted, adoring our little sparring matches. "But I didn't leave a card for you, nor did I orchestrate a trap. While I might enjoy taunting you, little slayer, I would never work with a hybrid."

"A hybrid?" she repeated, her eyes widening. "Oh my God, you're right. That's what he was—a hybrid between a shifter and a vampire. I didn't even know that was a thing."

"Apparently it is," I replied, stepping toward her. "And this one has a penchant for making a mess, something you know I would never do."

The purple rings around her pupils seemed to throb as she tilted her head back to assess my features. "You didn't leave the card?"

"I already said I didn't."

"And you didn't set the trap tonight?"

"Don't you think I would have been there sooner had I

arranged all of that?" I asked her, arching a brow. "You know how much I like to watch you squirm. Why would I miss all the fun?"

"There were probably cameras."

"Probably," I agreed. "But the feed wouldn't be available in our home realm."

That grabbed her attention. "You… you were…?"

"In our home reality," I answered for her. "Yes."

"You can go back," she whispered. Not a question, but a statement.

"I confirmed that for you yesterday."

"I know. But… I… I don't know if I believe you."

"Now who's playing a game?" I asked her, walking her back into the stone wall with one hand on her hip. I rested my opposite arm across the wall over her head, caging her in. "Ask me to prove it. I dare you."

She shivered. "You can take me back?"

"I can," I whispered. "And I will."

Her palms went to my chest, her eyes flaring wide. "What? No!" Alarm cascaded over her features, her pulse a racing temptation against her neck. "Shit, that's been the plan all along, wasn't it? To force me to go back and make me see whatever Dimitri has done to the world? The world I failed by not finding a way to return?"

If she was acting right now, I'd give her every award in the damn book. Because she appeared shell-shocked and broken, her expression one I'd dreamed of inspiring for nearly a century. Yet seeing it now did nothing for me.

"What do you think Dimitri has done to our world?" I asked her, genuinely curious. It seemed like such a strange thing to fear. If anything, she should be horrified by Grigori's antics, not my cousin's.

"I imagine he destroyed it after removing all the slayers in existence," she said, swallowing. "And you probably helped him. Did you enslave the human race? Turn them into walking blood bags?"

"You think I would do that?" I asked her, seeing the truth of it in her gaze. "Jesus, you do think I would do that." I frowned. "We loved each other once, Kseniya. You *knew* me. How could you possibly think I'd do such a thing?"

She shook her head slowly. "But it was all a lie."

"Was it?" I demanded. "Is that your way of confessing?"

Now it was her turn to frown. "Confessing what?"

"That you gave me up to Grigori. Traded my life for yours."

She gaped at me. "What the hell does Grigori have to do with this?"

"He has *everything* to do with this." My grip tightened against her hip. "Tell me what happened that night. Tell me *your* version."

"My version?" The water pouring around us didn't drown out her squeak of surprise—a squeak that morphed quickly into rage. "Are you fucking kidding me? You want me to tell you what happened? You *know* what happened, Cassius. You *used* me. I gave you everything, and you betrayed me in the worst way, laying all those deaths at my feet." Tears gathered in her eyes. "All because I thought I loved you." She tried to shove me away. "Fuck you, Cassius. *Fuck. You.*"

I caught her wrists, bringing them down to her sides as I pressed my thighs to hers.

"You think I betrayed you? Yet you were the one who gave me up to Grigori."

"Gave you up, how?" she demanded, her anguish palpable and heart-wrenching. "Is that why you gave Dimitri the secret passages? Because you thought I gave you up somehow?"

I gaped at her. "I didn't tell anyone about the passages. Well, no, Dimitri knew, but not because I told him."

"Sure." She rolled her eyes. "So he just happened to know how to get into the palace via the tunnels all on his own. You expect me to believe that?"

"I do, yes. He's old as fuck and knew all about the secret system below Romanov Palace. Hell, he told me about them before I even met you. How do you think I escaped you all those times we played?"

She gaped at me. "What?"

"You didn't show me the tunnels, sweet slayer. You may think you did, but I already knew about them. The only path you introduced me to was the one that led directly to your quarters, but I would have found it on my own eventually."

A myriad of emotions filtered through her pretty face, her nostrils flaring. "But if you already knew…"

I waited for her to finish, yet nothing else came, her mouth working soundlessly without words.

"Why are you so bothered by Dimitri knowing the tunnels?" I asked her, my grip on her wrists easing. "Why does it matter?"

"Because he used that knowledge to kill them all."

My forehead crinkled. "Kill who all?"

"The Romanovs."

"The Romanovs?" I blinked, my mind working rapidly over the information. Then my lips parted. It dawned on me then, the truth that she seemed to believe. "You think Dimitri led the revolution. That's why you keep commenting on him being king and destroying the slayer lines." Of course. How had I been so blind?

But if all that were true, then the story Grigori had given me was absolutely a lie.

Unless he'd convinced her of this truth, thereby persuading her to trade my life for hers.

I lifted my palm, wrapping it around her throat to seize and hold her gaze.

"Tell me the truth, Kseniya," I said, memorizing her face and listening closely to her heartbeat. "Did you work with Grigori to have me imprisoned? Did you trade your freedom for my life?"

"Imprisoned?" she breathed, her pulse skipping to an unsteady rhythm. "I don't...? What freedom? What are you talking about?"

I could see it there in her eyes—the lack of a lie. The clear confusion over my words. The uncertainty of my proclamations.

How she looked at me now was how I'd just looked at her seconds before when I couldn't understand her accusations regarding the tunnels.

We both had it all wrong.

There wasn't a need to take her home now.

I already knew the truth.

Neither of us had betrayed the other. Rather, we'd been played against one another, our minds overruling our hearts and souls and creating a disastrous fate.

"Fuck," I whispered, pressing my forehead to hers, uncertain of what to even say. So I kissed her instead.

Because I didn't trust my mouth to do anything else.

Not after everything I'd done and said to her already.

The hatred I felt for her died on a breath, replaced by the agony of realizing how badly I'd screwed this up. Had I just spoken to her from the beginning...

No. I couldn't go there. There was no changing the past, and dwelling on it wouldn't do either of us any favors.

Instead, we needed to move forward.

To make amends. To rewrite our future. To find the right path again.

"Cassius." She tried to push me away, but I kissed her harder. And she capitulated on a groan, her hands sliding upward to my shoulders, her arms wrapping around my neck.

Our mouths were done speaking.

It was time for our bodies to do the talking for us, to heal a century-old ache that had festered and burned between us for far too long.

We could work out the details later.

# VIØLET

## CHAPTER FOURTEEN

HEAT THREATENED to suffocate me from the inside out. I couldn't breathe around it, my heart a thundering rhythm in my ears that refused to abate.

Cassius had kissed me several times over the last few days, but none of those kisses had been anything like this.

He was branding me.

Claiming me.

*Owning* me.

And I was helpless to stop him, my body caving to his will despite my mind's protests.

What did he mean about being imprisoned? Why did he think I'd traded my life for his? What did Grigori have to do with any of this? And Dimitri knew about the tunnels before? Cassius knew, too?

My head spun with so many questions and uncertainties; all the while, Cassius possessed me with his mouth and touch.

Fuck, I'd missed this. Missed *him*. I'd dreamt of him so many times over the years, his soul permanently imprinted on mine no matter how hard I tried to forget him.

His blood provided a warmth inside me that responded to the familiarity of our past. His tongue taunted mine into a duel I had no desire to win. And his hands rooted me in the present, forcing me to accept how badly I still wanted him, even after everything we'd been through.

"I still hate you," I breathed against his mouth.

"Then hate-fuck me," he countered, releasing my throat to grab my hips.

I groaned at the thought, my nails digging into his shoulders. "Did your date last night not please you?" I asked, searching for ammunition and words to throw at him, to make this stop before I lost myself to him completely.

"No, she didn't please me at all," he replied, his teeth dragging along my lower lip. "She was too busy fingering herself into a coma while I stood outside her building. Then she went to bed and dreamt of me fucking another woman, yet in truth, I went home alone."

My brow furrowed. "What?" *He didn't fuck someone else last night?* Just the thought had my heart skipping a hopeful beat, which was exactly the opposite of what I'd intended to inspire with my barbed comment regarding his *date*.

"Compulsion hurts," he whispered. "So does being accused of using such a tactic against the love of my life." He kissed me again, his tongue punishing and cruel and deliciously wicked.

I groaned, an inferno building inside me that threatened to shatter every notion within my mind. Cognitive reasoning continued to slip, the apex between my thighs dampening with more than just water from above.

It'd been so long since a man had made me feel like this.

"Do you feel compelled right now, Kseniya?" His lips brushed my cheek on his way down to the pulse point of my neck. "Am I forcing your heart to race?" He slid his thigh between mine, angling upward. "Is your body rocking into mine because I told it to?"

I swallowed, a quiver gracing my spine as his fangs skimmed my throat.

"Answer me," he demanded, nipping my tender skin.

"No," I managed to reply, my voice hoarse with *need*. "Not compelled."

He laved the sensitive point, his bite imminent. He wouldn't ask; he'd take. Because he knew I'd give him permission anyway. Even now, hating him as I did, I would allow him to pierce me in whatever way he desired.

He had always been mine, just as I would always be his.

Which only made me despise him more.

And love him.

I nearly sighed, the conundrum in my head fracturing beneath an intoxicating cloud of bliss as his incisors slid inside me. His name left my mouth as a prayer, the endorphins of his bite sending a shock wave of pleasure to my core.

It'd been so long—*too long*—since I'd experienced such rapture.

All the hatred and pain melted away, his body a balm to the numerous aches and bruises left inside and out. He grabbed my hips, lifting me up against him. I wrapped my legs around his waist on impulse alone, his elongated shaft sliding through my slick folds.

*This*, I thought, delirious. *I need this.*

Every part of me burned for him, begging him to reclaim me in every way. Instead, he released my neck, his tongue tracing a path up my neck to my ear. "You're soaked for me," he whispered, pressing his length against me and hitting my clit with the bulbous head. "Tell me you missed me."

"No."

"Tell me how much you want this, Kseniya."

"No."

He chuckled, his teeth grazing my earlobe. "Always so stubborn."

"I hate you." It came out on a whimper as he slid against

me once more, his cock a torture device he wielded with expert precision.

"If I find out you're playing with me—that all of this is a game—I will kill you," he threatened, causing my legs to tighten around him. "No more foreplay. No more tricks. I'll end you, Kseniya."

"You'll try," I replied, arching into him, needing more friction, requiring more of *him*.

"I'll succeed."

"Fuck me, Cassius," I demanded, tired of the riddles and the verbal sparring and the torment. "Just take me."

His mouth sealed over mine, his hands gliding up my sides to cup my breasts and pinch the nipples between his thumbs and forefingers. He gave them a slight tug, knowing I desired a little pain with my pleasure. But he didn't give me what I wanted most. He just continued to lubricate himself, driving me mad with each subtle shift of his hips.

I dug my nails into his shoulders. "Stop teasing me."

"No." He used the same tone I had moments ago, then smiled against my lips before driving his tongue inside to skillfully dominate mine.

I shook against him, capitulating to his every whim. All I knew was Cassius. His touch. His mouth. His taste. His *heat*.

"*Cassius*." It came out as a curse, or maybe a prayer, my entire being inflamed with a craving only he could fulfill. He continued his assault below, both with his cock and his hands, touching me and stroking me and reducing me to a wanton female dying to be fucked.

"Tell me how you want it, baby," he said against my mouth. "Tell me how to fuck you."

It was on the tip of my tongue to reject him, to continue the verbal war we'd started. But I was too lost to the sensation to even try. "Violent," I replied instead. "Harsh. Make it hurt. Remind me why I hate you."

He hummed in approval, his resulting kiss a savage promise underlined in severity and bordering on cruel.

Passion thrived between us—a passion inspired by the deep-seated wrongness of our connection. The devastation of our past. The ensured destruction of our future.

I loathed him with a fiery energy that seared my very soul, yet craved him more with every inhale. "Now, Cassius."

"Only because you want it to hurt," he murmured, his hips gliding against mine. I didn't understand what he meant until the head of his cock found my entrance and drove inside.

A scream lodged in my throat, the impact of his thrust shooting off stars behind my eyes. "*Fuck.*" I'd forgotten how his size affected me, why I always preferred foreplay first. He hadn't expanded me to accommodate him, just took what had always belonged to him, and burned me with every inch of that impressive length. And he didn't give me a moment to acclimate, meeting my request with savage thrusts meant to bruise.

This was a punishment wrapped up in ecstasy. A mutual abhorrence punctuated by longing.

I did miss him. So damn much. Every muscled inch of his perfection. Each possessive touch. And that sinful mouth.

*Oh, God, yes.*

He knew exactly how to take me, how to complete me, how to destroy me, all in the same breath. I allowed it because there was no other option.

No. That wasn't true.

I allowed it because I wanted it. Wanted him. Wanted *this*.

His mouth ravaged mine, his grip arduous, his pace intense. I met him with each thrust, crying out in anguished rapture, biting him in a silent demand to stop while encouraging him with my nails against his neck.

It was chaos in its purest form. A dark dance of fate intertwined with death and utter desolation.

Resentment simmered beneath my skin.

Love pulsed in my heart.

Antagonism lashed out through my tongue.

Adoration sang to him from my soul.

His hand slipped to my core, his thumb finding my clit and circling it with a reverence that belied his fierce pace. It was barbaric and perfect and asinine.

And exactly what I needed.

My lower belly curled in anticipation, my legs quivering around him as I clamped my thighs down in a ferocious hold. There was no escaping me. No retreating now. No turning back from the cataclysmic turn of events.

We were going down together.

As a unit.

To burn in the fiery pits of despair as two star-crossed lovers who never should have indulged in this wicked affair.

"Now, Kseniya," he demanded, his words speaking to the part of my soul that bowed to his superiority.

Even after all these years, I couldn't disappoint him, couldn't deny him, couldn't stand up and take charge.

He'd possessed me from the very first day we met, those sinful silver eyes gleaming with a desire that rivaled my own. I'd knelt for him then, just as I'd kneel for him now.

My inner walls squeezed, my bloodstream spiking with adrenaline and sending me straight to hell on a scream that resembled his name.

My Cassius.

My enemy.

My lover.

*Mine.*

Tears streamed from my eyes, the pleasure too much, the

passionate inferno threatening to swallow every bit of my resolve and shatter me into exquisite pieces of ash.

Only, he followed me over that precipice, joining me in my agony, his own growl a benediction of sorts that tied us together in the abyss.

My limbs quivered with the release, my stomach cramping deliciously as wave after wave of euphoria rolled through each of my senses, drowning me in an enchanted sea.

It was so peaceful here.

So calm.

No sparring or verbal wars. No grating emotions. Just a joyful existence humming with electricity and grace.

Maybe I was dead.

I couldn't see anything, only a black, starless night with a light mist. A sigh escaped me, my forehead meeting a hard shoulder. *Cassius.* His fingers were combing through my hair, cherishing me with each stroke.

He held me so close, caressing me with such care, I longed to weep.

The scent of peppermint shampoo met my nose. I inhaled deeply, indulging in the fragrance, then sighed once more as he continued to brush through my tangled strands.

Some part of me recognized that he was bathing me now, his cock still lodged inside me as he held me up against the wall. It was unmistakably intimate, and while I should have fought it, I just didn't have the energy to try. So I reveled in it instead, warming beneath his sensual touch.

The soap reminded me of him, the cinnamon and ginger fragrance one I always associated with Cassius.

It wrapped around me, creating a blanket of security and comfort that I couldn't help but accept.

"I'm sorry," he whispered, his lips near my ear.

*For what?* I wanted to ask, but I was too lost in the bliss of his petting to try. Instead, I relaxed against him, allowing him to take complete control.

I must have dozed on his shoulder, because I awoke to the sensation of cotton against my skin, a soft towel wiping away the droplets of water and leaving me dry on the counter.

My eyes met his briefly, his lips curling into a knowing smile as I watched him pat himself dry, his arousal hanging prominently between his legs.

We were going to fuck again.

I could see it in his expression, feel it in my bones.

I welcomed it, accepting his hand as he led me to his bedroom and up into his four-poster bed. But as he entered me this time, it was slower. More thorough. A new memory engraved into my heart.

He didn't rush it, didn't make this time hurt, but instead soothed every ache inside me with his thorough pace.

More tears escaped my eyes, each one caught by his mouth.

He was making love to me in his own way, reminding me of what we used to have. I recognized it as a torment, one he would use against me when we awoke and he took it all away again. But I granted myself the indulgence, seeing this as a moment of closure.

We loved each other once.

This was what it had felt like.

And tomorrow, we would return to our fight. It would hurt. Mostly because I'd allowed this moment to happen.

I'd hate myself for it. Hate him even more, too.

Even after everything he'd done to me, I couldn't say no to him. I didn't *want* to refuse him. And perhaps that made me a fool.

However, for tonight, I'd remember who we once were. I'd dream of a different path. I'd lose myself to the hope of an alternate existence.

"I love you," I admitted, arching up into him. "But I also hate you."

"I know," he replied, kissing away yet another tear. "And I missed you, Kseniya."

"I missed you, too."

His mouth sealed over mine, speaking words with his tongue instead of his voice.

So much love.

So much pain.

So much fury.

I returned it all in kind, my arms around his neck, my legs cradling his. I welcomed him into me, opened my heart for just the night, and allowed this man to consume me entirely.

*Until morning*, I promised myself. *Only until morning.*

# CASSIUS

## CHAPTER FIFTEEN

SUNLIGHT SPILLED over my black silk covers, illuminating the gorgeous female beside me. The gem of her amulet glistened, drawing my gaze to her breasts. Her rosy nipples beaded alluringly in the cool morning air. I bent to capture one with my teeth, stirring a moan from my still-sleeping slayer.

I wasn't ready to embrace the new day yet, as I knew what it would bring.

Everything would either end for good between us or begin again.

Because I'd meant what I'd said—if I found out all of this had been a ruse on her part, I'd kill her. No more games. No more torment. Just sweet, blissful death.

But before we ventured into that dark territory, I wanted to taste her, to provide us both with a sensual memory to last a lifetime.

If this was my last time touching her, I needed to make it count.

I trailed my mouth down her flat stomach to her shaved mound, and lower to the glistening folds between her thighs. My name fell from her lips, her eyes still closed as though lost to a dream.

I smiled, pleased that her fantasy included me. I'd ask her later to tell me about it. And if she proved herself to be truthful, then I'd indulge her in as many of those visions as she pleased.

Her back arched as I grazed her clit with my nose. *Mmm.* My eyes momentarily closed at the beautiful aroma of her mounting arousal, my tongue begging for a taste. But I didn't give in to the desire. I wanted to draw this out, to tease her with my breath, and see just how wet she would become before she woke.

I ran my fingers up her thighs, my body settling between her legs.

Goose bumps pebbled along her skin, her forehead creasing as another moan spilled from her mouth.

"Cassius," she exhaled, her muscles tightening around me. "Please."

"Begging me even in your dreams," I replied. "That's my good little slayer." She knew how I adored watching her plead with me to take her, to fuck her, to give her the pleasure she so badly needed.

Kseniya shivered, another delectable sound gracing the air, followed by an incoherent mumble that sounded a little bit like a curse.

I chuckled against her pussy, purposely close enough to vibrate her sensitive bud. She jolted, a groan escaping her as her eyelashes began to flutter. Her hand slipped down her abdomen toward me, only to freeze upon finding me between her thighs.

Beautiful purple irises fixated on me, her pupils blowing wide. "Cassius."

"Yes, sweetheart?" I asked, bending to nibble her swollen nub.

She jolted beneath me, her gasp music to my ears. "Oh, *fuck.*"

"No, I intend to lick," I corrected her, demonstrating with a firm stroke between her folds. Her fingers went to my hair, clutching my white strands and holding me to her as she wantonly raised her hips.

"More."

Normally, I'd punish such a demand, but in this case, I agreed too much to deny her. Because now that I had her taste on my tongue, I needed more. Just as she said. And so I indulged myself, greedily memorizing her with my mouth and intimately kissing the female I considered mine.

She writhed beneath me, thoughts of our pending doom nowhere near her mind. I loved that I could do that—force her to fall into the pleasure and ignore everything else.

Her grip tightened as she tried to guide me to the place she desired, her yearning a hot wave in the war that went straight to my dick. I was already hard, but hearing her heartfelt mewls made me throb for her.

But I wanted to feel her come first.

I needed her to saturate my tongue, to provide a sensory memory to last a lifetime.

So I drove her over the edge with my mouth, my fangs skimming her clit to give her the slight pinch of pain I knew she craved. And then she fell apart beneath me, her grip tight and harsh against my head as she rode my mouth to oblivion.

It was fucking erotic as hell. I nearly came just from watching her. In this state, she cared about no one other than us, her focus entirely on the pleasure and none of the outside noise.

I didn't allow her to leave that state, instead crawling up her body and sliding home inside her in one quick thrust. She cried out at the intrusion, then captured my mouth with her own in a furious kiss meant to bruise.

This was my Kseniya, my wildcat, my perfect killer. She fought me every step of the way, her hips pushing against mine to force me to my side and my back as she settled on top of me.

I let her ride.

I let her fly.

I let her do whatever the fuck she wanted because in this state, she was glorious and hypnotic and so damn beautiful it hurt my heart.

She sat up, her breasts bouncing with each shift of her hips, her pace one I'd taught her long ago. Her nails bit into my chest, her eyes wild as though lost to her dreams. And maybe she was. Maybe she thought this was all in her mind. Somehow that made it even hotter, knowing that this was her unhinged and unguarded.

Her pussy began to tighten around me, another orgasm mounting inside her. I sat up, taking back her control by wrapping her hair in my fist and forcing her to kiss me. She growled and I snarled back. Then I flipped her off of me and onto her knees.

She tried to fight again, but I caught her hips and mounted her from behind, dominating her in the best way.

This woman loved power exchange, her independent soul craving a break in her steadfast control. I gave that to her now, taking away her choices and guiding her toward the cliff of no return.

She bent forward, her fingers gripping the bed as she accepted my powerful thrusts. I reached around her to thrum the place I knew she needed to be touched. Kseniya groaned in response, her body vibrating with need below mine as I drove her headfirst into ecstasy.

"Cassius!" She practically shrieked my name, her arms giving out from the onslaught of her orgasm. I caught her around her stomach just as my shaft pulsated, my seed erupting inside her and drawing a guttural sound from my throat.

I buried my face in her neck, prolonging our joined

climax with several more deep thrusts, before finally caving to the rapture and falling to the bed with her beside me.

We panted heavily, her back to my front and my arm still tight around her.

For minutes, or perhaps hours, we lay there, saying nothing and feeling everything.

We both knew what came next, and neither of us wanted to spoil the moment.

If Kseniya had thought she was dreaming before, she knew now that it was real. Which explained the stiffness in her shoulders and the sense of dread hanging over us.

"One more minute," I whispered against her neck. "Then we'll begin."

"Okay," she replied, understanding what I meant.

I didn't count the seconds. Instead, I enjoyed our final blissful moment of peace. I kissed the sensitive space behind her ear. I nuzzled her hair. I just held her.

Then I sighed. "Tell me your version of that night." She hadn't fully explained it before, only hinting at what she thought had happened. "What do you think I did?"

She didn't try to move away from me. Nor did she attempt to argue. She merely told me her version of what happened that night, stating I'd provided Dimitri with the secret tunnels and granted him entry into the palace to help him annihilate all the slayers. "Which is why you're here now," she concluded. "To finish the job."

I stayed silent for a heartbeat, contemplating her side of things. Her pulse had remained steady through her statement, lending credence to her belief in it being the truth. But it infuriated me that she thought I'd betray her in such a way. "If I wanted you dead, little slayer, you'd already be dead."

"You want me to suffer first, just like the Romanovs."

"Oh, they're suffering," I agreed. "But not because of my desires or plans."

I released her and rolled off the bed. There was only one way to solve this. She needed to *see*. Nothing I said would convince her. I also wanted to observe her reaction to what I revealed, to test the truthfulness of her words.

Kseniya watched me as I pulled on a pair of jeans and a shirt. Then she frowned as I tossed her a shirt and a pair of boxers. She was tiny enough that the latter would resemble shorts on her. "Put those on."

"Why?"

"Because I want to show you something." I grabbed a pair of shoes and socks, then looked at her. "Unless you want to remain naked. I'm fine with that, but you may wish you'd taken me up on the clothing offer after you see where we're going."

"Where are we going?"

"Put on the clothes, Kseniya," I said, leaving her to check on Luci. The hellhound had taken over my leather couch, her head propped up on a pillow as I entered. She wagged her tail slowly, then glanced pointedly at the arm she'd left on the floor beside her. "Good girl."

She snorted.

"Do you want to come with us or stay here?" I asked.

She perked up slightly, then canted her head.

I showed her my ring. "Portal jump."

She stood up and stretched out her front legs, then her back, before lazily climbing off the leather. I narrowed my gaze at the spot, noting the singe marks. "Did you burn my couch?"

Her tail wagged a little, her expression unapologetic.

Well, I'd only told her not to eat the bone on my furniture. I didn't say anything about burning it.

With a sigh, I returned to the bedroom and found

Kseniya dressed in my clothes, her hair deliciously rumpled from our night of sex.

Yeah, I'd be leaving her in that state. "Do you need anything before we go?" I asked her.

"My phone and a stake would be great," she drawled.

"I was referring to coffee or breakfast." I glanced at the windows, noting the time. "Or lunch." With her amulet around her neck, she wouldn't require as much food, but I wanted her comfortable.

"How about you tell me where we're going instead?" she suggested.

"To the past," I informed her softly, speaking in nonliteral terms. We wouldn't actually be going back in time, just to our true reality. "So you can see my version of events from that night."

Her jaw ticked. "Was that the point of all this? To lull me into a sense of contentment through sex, just to throw me back into hell? To show me an evening of fake kindness, only to rip it all away again?" She laughed without humor, muttering to herself, "Of course, I knew that was the plan, just as I knew this would hurt. But I just had to experience it, didn't I?"

"You have a very low opinion of me," I noted dryly. "Which I suppose I've earned over the last few days, but the past transgressions you hold against me are very wrong. I didn't show Dimitri the tunnels. As I said last night, he already knew. Just as I already knew about them."

"And next you'll tell me you didn't attack the palace. But I saw you that night, Cassius. Your eyes were crazed with bloodlust. You wanted me dead."

"I wanted to *save* you," I corrected on a low growl, furious at her for believing such a sordid version of events. "When I heard what was happening, I ran straight to you. If you saw anything *crazed* in my expression, it was the thought that I had arrived too late. But you weren't there. Instead, Grigori Rasputin was waiting for me."

She narrowed her gaze. "Sure. Okay. We'll pretend I believe that for a minute. So what did Grigori want?"

"The throne," I answered simply.

"What throne?"

"Dimitri's throne." I studied her, watching the disbelief filter through her pretty features. She truly believed her version of events over mine. Which meant she hadn't lied at all, that we'd both read this situation entirely wrong. "I can prove it, Kseniya."

"By taking me back," she replied. "You expect me to fall for that?"

"I expect you to give me a chance to explain the truth. If I wanted you dead, you'd be dead."

"That's not how you play the game, Cassius. You draw it out to inflict the maximum amount of pain imaginable, then you end it."

"True," I agreed. "But I'm not playing a game with you."

"You're always playing a game with me," she argued, throwing her hands outward. "You set all this up just to fuck with my head. *Again.*"

"And what do I win?" I asked her. "What do I gain from 'fucking with your head'?"

"Pleasure in my agony."

"I'd rather absorb that through sex," I tossed back. "Next reason, please."

She placed her hands on her hips, her expression infuriatingly stubborn. "I'm the last Romanov alive, right? You get the joy of tormenting the final heir, like some sort of trophy to parade around in our old world."

"You're not the last Romanov alive," I corrected her. "Not even close."

That gave her pause. "What?"

"You also wouldn't be much of a trophy since you're a cousin, not a direct descendant," I added. "If I wanted power or a medal of vampire honor, I wouldn't be here tracking you down. I came here to settle a revenge debt, one I thought I was owed. But I'm beginning to see that it was all a lie, a way to drive a wedge between us. Something I should have suspected, considering the source, yet here we are."

"Go back to the part about me not being the last slayer alive," she said. "Did others survive?"

This was the moment of truth. The Kseniya I once knew would react a very specific way to this information. I felt it to my very soul, that this was our pivotal sequence. How she reacted now would tell me everything I needed to know.

"Yes." I didn't elaborate on who had survived because only one person would truly matter to her. "Anastasia survived."

# CHAPTER SIXTEEN

*ANASTASIA SURVIVED.*

The two words repeated through my mind, circling with the phrase *He's lying. He has to be lying.*

This was all just a ruse to convince me to go back with him.

*But what if it's not? What if she's really alive?*

I shivered at the thought, my stomach clenching at what that implied. It would mean that I'd abandoned her all these years, thinking she was dead. Not that I could have returned even if I'd wanted to, but I would have tried harder had I known.

Cassius's comments about the last hundred years continued to plow through my head. Something about imprisonment and me trading my life for his. He kept talking about Grigori, too.

It was all so backward from what I believed, but I hadn't been there to watch it all play out. We'd escaped.

What if he spoke the truth?

What if I had this all wrong?

"She's… she's alive?"

"Yes." His eyes gave nothing away, those silver orbs almost appearing bored. But I felt the scrutiny behind his gaze. He was watching me for a reaction; I just didn't know what one he expected me to give.

I sat down on his bed, my legs suddenly unsteady. "How?" I asked, my voice as weak as I felt. "Did she escape?"

He gave a humorless laugh. "No. Only the three of you managed that. Not even I escaped."

I frowned. "What do you mean?"

He leaned against the door frame, his hands in his pockets as he casually crossed one ankle over the other. "I used the tunnels that night to try to find you. I went straight to your room, which Grigori had turned into a trap. One of his lieutenants shot me in the heart. I woke up in his dungeon, where I remained imprisoned for nine decades. It's not a pretty story."

This was what he'd referenced last night. But I still didn't understand. "Why would he imprison you?" The better question would be, *How did he accomplish such a feat?* Cassius was a royal. His kind would consider him untouchable.

"There's so much you don't know," he said softly. "Starting with what really happened that night. Dimitri didn't attack the Romanovs, Kseniya. Grigori did. It was a power play to overtake my cousin's throne. And he won."

"Grigori," I repeated, doubtful. "You expect me to believe that Grigori overpowered Dimitri?"

"I can prove it."

"Yeah, by taking me to our home realm," I guessed. "How convenient."

"Dimitri's intentions to negotiate peace with the Romanovs created dissension among the ranks. Grigori took advantage of that dissension. He orchestrated an attack, utilizing human and nonhuman contacts, in an effort to show that he could finish the job my cousin refused to start."

Cassius pushed off the door frame and stalked toward me.

"You can choose not to believe me, Kseniya. But it doesn't change the fact that your best friend is trapped in a hell she can't escape from."

"What are you talking about?"

"Grigori kept her for himself," he said, stopping in front of me. "Rumor has it that she's his pet assassin. But no one knows where she is. Which is why Sapphire—a witch, very much like your Roskana—is busy trying to locate her. I can prove all of this with a single visit, Kseniya."

He held out his hand, the offer clear.

This could all be some sort of elaborate trap meant to hurt me emotionally, in addition to physically. Because if anyone could set the terms of this devious game, it would be Cassius.

Yet I couldn't detect any amusement in his features. With his wild white hair, he appeared disheveled. Unkempt. So very unlike the Cassius of my past. He almost seemed... tired.

"I won't force you, Kseniya, even though we both know I could," he added softly, his hand hanging between us. "At one point in our history, you trusted me. I'm asking you to do it again. Just for today. Let me show you the truth, just as you've shown me."

"What truth have I shown you?" I wondered out loud.

"That you had no idea I was imprisoned for nine decades. That you never gave me up to Grigori. And perhaps the most telling truth—that you really don't know how to travel the realms. Because if you did, you wouldn't mind going with me now. You have your portal key, slayer. It's hanging around your neck."

I frowned down at my amulet. "It doesn't work like that. Rowan and I have tried."

"It does work like that," he corrected. "You just don't know how to use it correctly." He sounded sad, causing my gaze to flicker back to his. "I spent so many years thinking you could return to me and chose not to. I realize now how wrong I've been."

"I wouldn't have returned to you," I told him. "Because you..." I trailed off, unable to utter the phrase with the conviction I once possessed.

"I never shared your secrets," he promised, lowering his hand to his side. "A slayer long before your time did. Dimitri's known about them for longer than you've been alive. Just as I did."

He crouched before me, looking up at me rather than down at me while I remained seated on the bed.

"I would never have betrayed you in that manner, Kseniya. And some part of you knows it, too. Which is why you let me touch you last night. Why you allowed me to love you. Why you're sitting there now, considering taking my hand." He balanced with his forearms on his thighs, the picture of ease. "Come with me, little killer. Let me show you the truth."

Luci picked that moment to snort from the doorway, her expression one of boredom. I swear she was saying, *Let's go already*.

Cassius grinned, likely reading the same thing I did from her big brown eyes. "Luci believes me."

My hellhound grunted and plopped her butt down, then cocked her head to the side while looking at me.

"You don't know him like I do," I told her.

I swore her eyes actually rolled.

"Pretty sure your hellhound is a good judge of character," Cassius drawled, standing once more to walk over and scratch her behind the ear. The little traitor leaned into him on a happy huff, urging him to continue. "You accepted me even when I wanted to kill your master."

She licked her chops at that yet somehow made the mannerism cute while leaning into him more.

"You're right," he whispered. "We both know I was never really going to hurt her." He patted her on the head and turned toward me again, waiting.

I swallowed, my instincts rioting in a myriad of directions. If I had my phone, I'd call Rowan for her advice.

Actually, no, I wouldn't. She'd tell me to get the hell out of there and to not look back.

*But what if he's right?* I wondered for the thousandth time. *What if Anastasia is alive?*

He'd claimed Grigori had her, just like he'd held Cassius prisoner.

"How could Grigori turn Anastasia into his personal assassin?" I asked, my brain finally catching up with everything Cassius had said. "She'd never agree to that."

"Compulsion," he replied. "*Intense* compulsion."

I shuddered at the thought, my mind turning over what Cassius had done to me just the other night. I'd been out of my mind with lust, unable to think for myself. It'd served as a stern lesson, one that confirmed he'd never compelled me before. Not like that.

My thumb grazed the tanzanite stone hanging from my neck, a memory of Rowan enchanting it to counter compulsion gracing my thoughts. That had occurred after we'd escaped. Because I'd thought Cassius had persuaded me with vampire magic to love him.

Rowan saw through it but allowed me my belief—a belief Cassius had single-handedly shattered in a night.

We were in love once. Might even still be in love now.

All these years I wanted to punish him, to kill him, to hate him for what he'd done to me. Then he showed up with this outlandish story, inspiring hope inside me that refused to die.

If he was telling the truth, then we could have a future

together. It would be harsh and riddled with a violent past, but that was how we thrived. Our passion had never been easy, the very notion of a relationship between us forbidden.

Yet at one point, I would have sacrificed everything for him.

Could I do that today? Could I sacrifice my pride on the mere glimmer of possibility that he might be telling me the truth?

He lifted his hand again, his silver eyes gleaming with promise.

"If this is all a ruse, I will find a way to end you," I vowed.

His lips curled. "Likewise, baby."

I nodded. "Then we have a tentative accord."

"Sounds familiar," he taunted.

Yes. It did. Because those were the exact words the Romanovs said to Dimitri when he proclaimed he wanted to strike a deal.

Only, this wasn't about an arrangement or temporary peace. This was about a potential path. A new destiny. A twist of fate I never saw coming.

With my heart in my throat—or perhaps on my sleeve—I stepped forward to press my palm to his. "Take me to the past."

"No," he said, pulling me into him. "I'm taking us to our future." His lips whispered across mine. "Let's go."

He brushed his thumb over the gem on his index finger, the ruby flaring to life as he murmured a word in Russian that meant "revenge." A portal opened, just like mine usually did, only the inside glittered like diamonds. Luci snarled at it, her fur lifting on end. I felt similarly, the energy surrounding the portal all wrong.

"Trust me," Cassius said, his silver irises locked on mine. "Please."

Luci grumbled, then bumped his leg as though to say, *Lead on.*

However, his gaze was on me, waiting.

It'd be so easy for him to throw me inside, to force me to comply. Yet he wanted me to choose this, to *trust* him, just like he requested.

My instincts flared, my heart panicking at the thought of how he might use this against me. But my soul urged me to take a step forward, to see where this went, to find out if he spoke the truth.

A part of me was curious. I *wanted* to know what had happened to my old world, to witness firsthand what I'd accidentally left behind.

With a decisive nod, I allowed that growing curiosity to inspire me forward and followed Cassius through the shimmering curtain of cool air. Magic pooled across my skin, shrouding my limbs in goose bumps. The cool stone beneath my feet reminded me that I was barefoot and wearing only Cassius's clothes.

I nearly turned back, wanting a strong shield for whatever awaited me on the other side, but the kiss of sand gave me pause.

*Black* sand.

I studied my feet, noting the dark, grain-like texture covering my soles. "Where are we?" I asked, lifting my gaze to find dark blue waters to my right and an estate of white walls to my left.

"The coast of Greece," Cassius replied, his hand still in mine. Luci stood a few feet ahead, her nose buried in the earth as she inhaled the foreign scent. Then she danced around, frolicking in the essence that matched her sable fur. I frowned as she darted into the ocean, her hellhound shape taking form as she sent the water up around her in a misty cloud.

"Huh," I said, surprised. "I had no idea she liked the ocean."

We'd never been, but from the look of it, Luci *loved* the water. She began to roll around, shifting between hellhound form and wolf form, her tongue hanging out of her mouth in a happy grin.

"What the fuck is that?" a deep voice demanded, causing my spine to stiffen.

*Dimitri, the king of vampire kind, is standing at my back.*

*Oh, shit…*

# CHAPTER SEVENTEEN

I TURNED SLOWLY, my heart firmly lodged in my throat. I had allowed Cassius to take me here unarmed and barely dressed. It was the worst decision of my life. And now I would face the strongest, most dangerous vampire in existence… without a stake.

Not that a stake would work on him.

No, Dimitri would require a different brand of death. One where I removed his head and burned his body. I could do a lot of things, but I wasn't sure I had that in me right now.

Part of being strong was knowing one's limits, and I knew mine very well.

The vampire king sauntered down the beach, his focus not on me but on Luci playing on the shore. His dark hair resembled waves in the warm breeze, his ocean-blue eyes glistening in the late afternoon sunlight. "Is that a hellhound?"

"Yep." Cassius grinned. "It's Kseniya's familiar."

"Seems appropriate," Dimitri drawled, stopping a few feet away from me.

His aristocratic features had hardened over the years, the perfect symmetry of his face somehow appearing more severe. The intensity increased as his gaze met mine, his pupils resembling dark pits of fury carefully contained by the tumultuous blue rim around them.

I swallowed, my pulse skipping a beat. Something I knew he noticed because his attention went momentarily to my neck before shifting to his cousin. "You tamed her."

Cassius snorted. "She's under the impression I've tricked her into coming here."

"Didn't you?" Dimitri asked.

"Not like I'd originally intended," Cassius admitted. "She didn't give me up to Grigori."

"You're certain?"

"Yes."

Dimitri nodded. "Good. Then perhaps you can stop sulking and figure this shit out." He stepped away from us and toward Luci.

I nearly went after him, intending to stop whatever he planned to do, only he went to his haunches and held out his hand to allow her to sniff him.

Luci shook out her coat, the black fur returning once more, and pranced over to him, her intelligent brown orbs accepting as she bumped his palm with her snout. He chuckled and ran his fingers over her dark head to scratch her behind the ear. "You'll be a fun addition," he said, seemingly pleased.

"Addition?" I said, my voice coming out with a slight croak from forgetting how to use it the last few minutes.

"Yes," he replied, glancing back at me with his fingers lost in Luci's fur. "Assuming you intend to stay and help us track down Anastasia? I imagine she'll appreciate having a familiar face once we break whatever compulsion she's currently under."

I blinked at him. "So it's true? She's alive?"

"Why would I make up such a tale?" he countered, giving me a look that said, *What a waste of time that would be.*

"Look around you," Cassius suggested. "Do you think we'd be hiding here if Dimitri were still leading the Vampire Dynasty? Where are all his royal guards? His mortal harem?"

Dimitri snorted. "I did not have a harem."

"You had several toys."

"Only for eating."

Cassius shrugged. "Fair. My point is, they're gone, as are all your guards." He returned his attention to me. "Is that what you expected, Kseniya? Or were you envisioning another sort of reality?"

I'd expected this world to resemble hell, to see humans enslaved and vampires overindulging in rivers of blood. Not a sandy shore on the coast of Greece.

Cassius was right. There were no guards or humble servants. No humans begging to be bitten. No wanton females playing chase. It was oddly peaceful here. Quiet.

*No, it's remote.*

The residence behind us was vast, but nowhere near the size of Dimitri's home palace. And it held a protective vibe, as though hidden by wards.

I slowly moved in a circle, taking in every angle, my mind confirming my thought. "This property is enchanted."

"Yes." Dimitri stood, the bottom of his black pants drenched with water and ruining his leather shoes. "We're in hiding."

"Why?" I asked, guessing at the answer but wanting to hear it from the man himself.

"Because I don't want Grigori to find me right now," Dimitri said. "I'm not ready to fight him yet."

"He took your throne the night of the attack." Not a question, but a statement, one I was beginning to believe.

"He stole my entire fucking kingdom," Dimitri replied. "And I've been preparing my next move ever since."

I'd say a century was a long time to plan, but Dimitri was

over a millennium old, perhaps closer to two millennia. He wouldn't see a hundred years as very long at all.

"It took a while to find all the players," Cassius added.

"Yes," his cousin agreed. "I had to rescue them from various places all over the damn globe because they weren't equipped to save themselves."

Cassius grunted. "Yeah, well, at least he didn't turn me."

"Remains to be seen," Dimitri murmured, turning away from us. "Try groveling, C. I hear that helps with women."

"Says the man who doesn't date."

Dimitri lifted a shoulder, continuing toward a path at the edge of the beach, not once looking back. "Let me know when she's ready to join us. We have shit to do."

"Yeah, yeah." Cassius drew his fingers through his hair, frowning as he found a knot.

I'd probably find a few in my own strands if I tried to finger-comb it, which was why I left it to hang around me in a mess of purple locks. I had no one to impress here. The only male I'd ever cared about stood beside me in an equally disheveled state.

"Want a tour?" he asked.

"I thought you were supposed to try groveling," I replied, feeling slightly more at ease now that Dimitri had left us alone. This could all still be a giant ruse, one meant to lull me into a comfortable frame of mind before breaking me, but the atmosphere out here felt too tranquil for that.

I wouldn't let my guard down yet.

But I would let Cassius show me around, see what other proof he had to offer that I'd gotten it all wrong.

The commentary on his imprisonment helped.

As did Dimitri's casual behavior. He hadn't seemed eager to kill me at all, just asked when I'd join them.

"What did he mean by that?" I asked, thinking out loud. "About joining you all?"

"He's planning a revolution," Cassius replied. "He intends to recruit Anastasia as well, which is why he's trying to find her."

"Why?"

"Because we're going to need all the help we can get to take Grigori down." Wariness overtook his features, mingling with an undertone of vengeance. I could almost taste the conflict on my tongue.

"Is this what you wanted to show me, Cassius?"

He blew out a breath, his face tilting back to observe the sky above for a long moment before returning his gaze to mine. "What I want is the truth. Grigori told me that you traded your freedom for mine, causing me to blame you for nine decades of torment, and if I'm honest, heartbreak, too. I thought you could return to me with your amulet and chose not to."

I followed his gaze to the gem hanging from my chain. "I don't think mine works that way."

"It does," he insisted. "You just don't know how to activate it, which proves you had no idea how to find me."

"If I had, I would have tried because I wanted to kill you," I admitted. "I've spent the last century hating you for betraying me."

"Except I didn't betray you, Kseniya. I tried to save you." He gestured around us. "This is my proof. Do you think we'd be here if Dimitri were still king?"

*No*, I wanted to say, but I couldn't. Agreeing with him would mean I believed him, and I wasn't quite there yet.

I'd lived with my hatred for so long that it was impossible to forget it, to allow something as simple as a beach to persuade me otherwise. Logically, I understood his point. Emotionally, I needed more.

He must have seen that resolve in my gaze, because he released another long breath, his shoulders falling.

"All right. Follow me," he said, not a request but a demand.

I glanced at Luci, her joyous smile telling me she had no interest in leaving the water anytime soon. She would trail after us when she was ready, then paw at any doors that stood in her way until they either opened or burned into a Luci-size hole.

"Dimitri has only been here for about a decade." He walked in the same direction his cousin had gone, his gait slow and steady and underlined in casual ease.

"Where was he before?" I wondered out loud. If Dimitri was in fact overthrown, then he couldn't have stayed in Russia.

"Silver Lake Pack," he replied. "In New York."

I blanched. "He stayed with the wolves?" Well, that was one place to hide. Grigori would never think to look there. Hell, no vampire would. The wolves weren't exactly allies of the Vampire Dynasty.

"He's been allying with supernats all over the world. Well, except the French Royals. They want fuck all to do with this war. The others are interested, though."

"How did he get the wolves to allow him to stay?"

"Nathan," Cassius replied. "Did you ever meet him? He was actually born in Russia, but before your time."

I shook my head. "I've never met a shifter, just know of them."

He gave me a look as we reached the back garden of Dimitri's estate. "Alaric's a shifter."

"Something I didn't know until last night."

"How the hell did you miss that? He reeks like a dog."

"I don't have your sense of smell."

"Clearly. But come on, he's even shaggy like a mutt. The man has 'alpha' written all over him."

I shrugged. "We've only ever sparred. Not fucked."

That caused Cassius to freeze midstep, his focus zeroing in on me. "It'd better stay that way."

I pretended to think about it. "Well, now that I know he's an animal, I may just want to take him for a ride."

"Kseniya."

"What?" I gestured between us. "It's not like we're an item."

His palm encircled the back of my neck, yanking me to him. "We're more than an item."

My hands met his chest, but rather than push him away, my nails dug into his cotton shirt. "I still hate you."

"You also love me."

"Do I?"

"You do," he assured me, all quiet confidence. "And I don't share."

"Neither do I," I returned, not really sure what we were declaring here but unable to hold back my tongue.

"Good."

"Good."

We stared each other down, the intensity between us sending a sizzle of energy across my skin and raising every hair along my arms. His irises smoldered, giving everything and nothing away at the same time.

It would be so easy for him to kill me. Right now. Right here. But I didn't fear him. I never really had, even when I knew he'd found me with the sole purpose of making me suffer. There'd always been this strange sort of understanding between us.

Was it possible that we'd gotten everything wrong? That we'd completely misread our situation?

*Yes*, I thought. We were both so stubborn, our resolves set within our own expectations. And it was just too easy to believe he'd betrayed me. Our relationship had never been grounded in a reality of equality. We were forbidden to one another. It was part of what made us burn so hot together.

We both thrived on the danger.

"I want a stake," I told him.

"Okay," he agreed.

I knew he'd give me one. Not because it would make me safe but because it would add threat to our situation.

Cassius liked risk.

As did I.

He released my neck to trail his fingers down my arm to my palm. He clasped my hand tightly and tugged me along beside him. There was a pool beyond the garden, framed by a deck of white cement. A patio surrounded the back of the house, littered with vacant chairs, and a myriad of doors that allowed various entry points into the estate.

Cassius chose the one in the middle, dragging me into a great room that boasted high ceilings and all modern furnishings.

Still no guards or humans.

Rather than head up, he pulled me down a hallway and toward the front door, then outside again. I didn't ask his intentions, choosing to admire the surroundings instead. Cobblestone streets, greenery, pretty flowers. Yeah, I could live here. It was peaceful and remote and warm. Very Mediterranean.

Cassius took me to a smaller house that seemed to exist within the property's perimeter but was much more quaint in stature.

He knocked once before entering, then led me through a smaller living area to a sunroom near the back. A woman with shocking blue hair sat in a recliner chair, her eyes closed. Her exposed legs were crossed at the ankles, her small feet dancing to a rhythm I couldn't hear.

Cassius released me to walk over to a stereo on a cabinet

beside her, his nimble fingers rolling the volume button downward. The female's eyes opened, not in alarm but in annoyance. "I wasn't done listening to that."

"I need your attention for a minute," he replied.

She pulled a pair of buds from her ears, her pretty face marred by a scowl. "It could have waited thirty more seconds."

He just looked at her.

"Fine." She rolled off her chair and left the room, not once looking my way.

"Okay," I said. "Why are we here?"

"You wanted a stake," he replied, leaning against the wall with his arms crossed. "She's grabbing you one."

"But you didn't even tell her we wanted one," I pointed out, confused as hell.

"She knows."

"I do," the blue-haired woman replied, handing me two stakes.

"Thanks," I said, baffled as to how she knew what I wanted. As I had nowhere to holster them, I held one in each palm.

"Hmm," she hummed, reaching for my amulet. I jumped away from her, only to find Cassius at my back. "I'm not going to take it," she told me, moving closer. "I just sense something strange. Something that wasn't there when I looked at it originally."

"Originally?"

"This is Sapphire," Cassius explained. "The one helping us locate Anastasia. She's also the one who found you."

"Roskana," she murmured. "I found Roskana's magic. But she's crafted an amazing trinket. It responds to your blood. I didn't notice that before because it wasn't active. How intriguing. The one I made for Cassius only allows him to jump realms. Yours provides protection in a multitude of ways. No wonder the others wanted Roskana to make more. Huh."

"The others?" I repeated.

She waved a hand. "Neither here nor there. Although, I think she's on her way here. No, not here, but sort of." She tapped her chin, taking several steps back. "Well, that should be fascinating indeed. Which path will she choose? The wolf says his, but she won't go quietly. How fun."

"What are you talking about?" I asked, perplexed by her nonsense.

"Sapphire often talks in riddles," Cassius said softly. "She has a knack for fortune-telling, but it's not an exact science."

"Yet I was right about you, wasn't I?" she mused, sounding proud. "You found your heart again, just as I predicted. Your vengeance belongs with Rasputin." She spat out the name, her blue eyes flashing with anger. "*Our* vengeance belongs with him, King of Vampires, imposter to the throne. We need Nikola. Yes. I will find her."

"Nikola?" I tried to look over my shoulder at Cassius, but Sapphire's sigh drew me back to her.

"Oh, yes. Slayer queen. Anastasia Nikola Romanov. She goes by Nik now. Hmm, crafty with a blade. Yes, very crafty with a blade indeed." Sapphire clicked a few buttons on her desktop monitor, then moved some items around on what resembled a chessboard. "We are close. Very, very close. May I go back to my music now?"

Cassius responded by walking over to her stereo and turning up the volume.

"Thank you, thank you," she chirped, sliding back into her recliner and placing the buds in her ears once more. Then she frowned and removed them, her eyes meeting mine. "I should have followed his soul. It's linked right to yours. Hmm. Anyway." She closed her eyes, her feet resuming their seated dance.

"That's probably all we're going to get out of her," Cassius muttered, stepping backward out of the room. "How do you feel about food? I know you're immortal again, but sustenance is still something you require, yes?"

"I do like to eat," I admitted. "But I would kill for a coffee right now."

His lips twitched. "There are a few cafes in town we can visit for a late lunch." He paused to glance out the windows behind Sapphire. "Actually, I suppose it'll be dinner, given the time change on this continent." He shrugged. "Anyway, we can talk more while you evaluate the truth of my claims."

In other words, he was giving me an opportunity to compare realms, to see how much of my original world rivaled the E.V.I.E. universe.

"Oh! I left a case in your rooms," Sapphire interjected. "It'll help."

"Help with what?" he asked, but she was already lost to her music again, ignoring us with her eyes closed once more. He sighed. "Right. Let's go clean up. Then we'll grab a bite and do some portal hopping."

# CASSIUS

## CHAPTER EIGHTEEN

THE CRATE ENDED up being a box of clothes and weapons for Kseniya. Everything fit her perfectly, including the holster around her right thigh. It didn't hold a gun, but special bullets meant to take down a vampire.

I hadn't been pleased with the gift. And I was certain Dimitri wouldn't approve.

However, I had to admit it looked sexy as hell strapped to Kseniya's leg. She hadn't bothered to hide it, the accessory pretty much blending in with her black jeans. If anyone noticed, they'd just assume it was a fashion aesthetic.

A gun and the two stakes from Sapphire were hidden beneath her leather jacket. And a knife was tucked into her boot.

She resembled a warrior.

*My* warrior.

In this mode, we'd be a pretty even match. I had every intention of asking her to spar after we were done exploring. She was still full of questions, our dinner together only skimming the surface of her inquiries. I'd explained that night from my point of view, revealing every painful detail. Her expression had given nothing away, but her eyes told me I was beginning to crack the ice of her resolve.

The ice melted further when I took her to New York City,

showing her the North American Shifter Council headquarters building that sat in place of her E.V.I.E. one.

Then we ventured all over the world so she could see that this realm wasn't much different from the one she'd lived in these last hundred or so years.

With a few exceptions, like the one before us now.

We were crouched outside the restored version of Romanov Palace, the grounds littered with human militia. Grigori hired them under the pretense of guarding a prison. However, inside lay a slayer camp.

"How many?" she asked in a low voice.

"I don't know," I admitted. "But whenever he discovers a new line with even the potential of holding a slayer gene, the family is shipped here."

What he did with them after remained a mystery.

"We believe Anastasia was trained here," I whispered. "But she was moved several decades ago and continues to be moved to keep her whereabouts unknown."

"Which is why Sapphire is tracking her," Kseniya translated.

"Yes. She's searching for her future location, not her current one, so we can grab her when she arrives." And then the real fun would begin.

Grigori knew that Dimitri was alive. No one had been able to claim the kill because no one had succeeded, and freeing me from jail a decade ago only further proved Dimitri's lively state.

What Grigori didn't know was our plan.

Kseniya vibrated, her anger a palpable wave, but she wasn't naive enough to think she could stop this all on her own. I saw it in her eyes when she looked at me, the resolve settling through her features. "He needs to pay."

"He does," I agreed. "And, unfortunately, this isn't the only thing he's done."

"Show me," she demanded.

I'd anticipated her saying that, which was why I already held my palm out for her to take. Three more sites were on our tour, all dangerous, and all depicting the new world order instituted by Grigori.

He hadn't necessarily enslaved the human race, but he had control over several diplomats throughout Eastern Europe. I showed her everything we knew about Grigori and his current regime, keeping to the shadows while she observed. She remained mostly quiet, watching and learning and seeing that the vampires in charge now were not the royals of her past.

We didn't go near Grigori. Just close enough to some of his minions to give her a better view of the world she'd left behind.

By the time we finished, she had tears in her eyes.

I opened a portal to take us back to my room. She didn't argue, just stepped through the threshold.

Luci stood on the other side waiting for us, her tail wagging excitedly at our arrival. She had a big bowl of water by the door—something that wasn't there when we left—and a half-eaten steak beside it.

"Dimitri fed you," I said, amused. He always did have a soft spot for animals.

The hellhound gave me a lopsided smile, her tongue flopping sideways out of her mouth.

Kseniya gave the hellhound a scratch behind the ear, then walked through the double doors to stand on the balcony just off my master suite.

I joined her, the two of us silent as the waves lapped at the shores below. The beach was entirely ours, Sapphire's magic extending to all angles of Dimitri's estate. While this was technically my stand-alone property, it was all connected. Just as Sapphire's small house sat within our perimeter.

A few others had homes nearby, all loyalists who desired Dimitri to retake his throne.

We were living proof that the size of the army didn't really matter. The power among us placed us on top. But my cousin didn't want to risk it yet. He didn't fight a battle unless he knew with certainty that every outcome was in his favor. And he wouldn't feel confident until he had Anastasia.

"I need to call Rowan," she said softly. "But I don't even know where to start. If she finds out we left Anastasia in that place when we could have helped her..." She trailed off, swallowing.

"There are a lot of things we could blame ourselves for, but that'll just make us feel worse and do nothing to solve the situation," I murmured. "The only antidote is to move forward, to take charge of the future and inspire change."

"Is that your way of telling me not to expect an apology from you?" she asked, rotating toward me.

"I've already apologized, Kseniya. I won't grovel."

"Maybe you should," she challenged.

"I could say the same to you," I countered, taking a step toward her. "You haven't even attempted to apologize, little killer."

Her jaw clenched. "I'm not the one who traveled the realms and threatened to destroy you."

"No, apparently, I'm slightly more dedicated to my vengeance than you are." It was a taunt. A cruel twist of words. A way to push her out of the mental trap threatening to consume her.

Wallowing in what-ifs would destroy her.

Yes, she'd missed the opportunity to save Anastasia before. But now she had a new chance to right the wrong. She just needed to be in the appropriate frame of mind to be successful.

Pitying herself and feeling bad about the past would weaken her, not strengthen her.

So I would push her.

Hurt her.

Force her to rebuild.

Because I knew that was what my slayer required.

"I'm not apologizing again, Kseniya," I reiterated. "You didn't die. You were barely even hurt. And besides, it's not my fault you've grown comfortable in your new little world. Yeah, I tormented you a bit. Then I made it all better with my cock." I stepped closer to her, allowing her to feel the heat of my body. "You should be thanking me, sweetheart. Not asking for another apology."

Her fingers curled into fists at her sides. "*Stop*."

"Stop what?" I asked her. "Stop speaking the truth? Stop showing you what really happened here? Stop making you see how wrong we had it? Stop forcing you to realize that self-pity won't do you a damn bit of good when your former best friend is being used as a weapon by a monster because you couldn't figure out how to return and save her?"

Kseniya whipped the stake out from inside her jacket so fast I was almost impressed. Except she aimed it right for my heart.

I dodged, tsking her in a taunting manner. "The wolf certainly didn't teach you any decent tricks while we were apart."

It felt good to insult the alpha male. Mostly because I didn't like the notion of him having his paws all over my slayer. Kseniya had stated they hadn't fucked, but that didn't mean my mind hadn't envisioned exactly what that would have entailed had they slept together.

She charged me, her rage pouring off her in intoxicating ripples that caused my blood to thump wildly in my veins.

This was what we needed.

A match.

A fight.

A violent bout of foreplay before I took her and claimed her as mine in every way imaginable.

She wanted an apology? Well, this was my version of it.

She needed an outlet, someone to blame, and I'd be that someone for her. I'd allow her to fight me, to bleed me, to do whatever she needed to rid herself of the guilt and pain of realizing how wrong she'd been.

When she swapped the stake in favor of the gun, I tackled her, grappling for control of the weapon that could seriously injure me. She growled, snarled, shrieked, and screamed.

I hoped like hell Dimitri didn't hear her. He wouldn't agree with my manner of therapy, particularly as it put my life in serious jeopardy. Because if anyone could kill me, it was the vixen beneath me on the ground.

Not only did she maintain the strength and skill, but I would consider allowing her to win. If I thought that was what she needed.

In this case, she'd hate herself if she succeeded, so I fought her.

I caught her wrist in my hand, squeezing tightly and forcing her to release the gun, then I rolled away from it and felt the point of a stake against my ribs.

She dug in enough to bleed, my reflexes not fast enough to catch her entirely. I cursed, not enthused by the sharp wooden spike drawing blood from my side. With a growl of my own, I shoved her off of me, then yanked the partially embedded stake and tossed it unceremoniously onto the balcony.

Kseniya was back up on her feet, resembling an outraged goddess with her purple hair wild and her irises swirling with stark ferocity. My dick reacted to the image, hardening in my slacks, eager to play.

This was our version of seduction.

As was evidenced by the faint aroma of her growing arousal.

I stood and removed my ruined suit jacket, throwing it over her gun to make it harder for her to retrieve it. Then I began to roll the sleeves of my shirt, feigning boredom. "I didn't realize you needed a breather between rounds, Kseniya. Out of shape?"

She narrowed her eyes. "You're an asshole."

"Yes," I agreed. *But I'm also yours, baby*, I clarified in my mind, smiling. "Come get me, little killer. Use that last stake and show me what you can do." She had a knife somewhere, too. Would she switch it up?

*Nope*, I thought, grinning as she twirled the wooden stake between her fingers.

She danced forward, light on her feet, and leapt to my left, then doubled back around to my right at the last second, her movements impressive and *fast*.

I spun, trying to dislodge her, only to feel the sharp point of her weapon against my sternum all over again, this time shoving inside and causing the breath to leave me on a whoosh of air.

*Fuck!*

I went to my knees, using my momentum to take her down with me.

She rolled, sending me to my back, her legs straddling my middle as she drove the stake in more.

Darkness blinked in and out of my vision for half a beat, just long enough for her to gain complete control.

A stake wouldn't kill me.

But the blade she pulled out to place at my throat could. Especially partnered with the gun that I suspected held some sort of fire-inducing bullet.

"I think it's time for you to apologize," she said, her

breath coming out in a pant, the dagger pressing hard enough to draw blood.

*Jesus Christ!*

My rib cage burned, my heart beating a chaotic rhythm underlined in fucked-up arousal and emphasized with true fear.

She'd bested me.

My little slayer had finally well and truly bested me. Perhaps because I'd been playing with her, but it didn't matter. She had my proverbial dick in her hands, squeezing it sharply and threatening to rip it off.

"Kseniya," I breathed, her name coming out on a sharp exhale choked by the blood trickling into my lungs.

Fuck, this was going to be a bitch to heal. But at least she didn't look like a wounded puppy anymore. No, she resembled my stunning slayer—savage and dark and empowered by the kill.

I coughed, the movement stirring a sharp sting at my throat where the blade cut deeper.

Her violet irises were wild, her supremacy a thrill.

Then she removed the knife to lick along the tip, tasting my blood. Her eyes closed, her thighs tightening around my torso.

I didn't move, too enthralled by the goddess straddling me.

It'd be so easy to take advantage of the moment, to grab the stake and yank it out of me, then overpower her and take that knife to do my own slicing and dicing. But I wanted to lose. Now that her emotional upheaval had subsided—replaced by a dangerous hunger for my blood—I could admire her and indulge in the moment.

She pressed the knife to my neck again, her opposite hand going to the stake. However, rather than driving it in deeper, she leaned down to kiss me. For a terrifying moment,

I thought she was saying goodbye, her intention to destroy me coming true.

Only, her tongue parted my lips to dip inside as she yanked the stake out of me. The knife left my neck as well, her body collapsing on mine as she indulged me in a kiss meant to ravage nations.

All her fight morphed into intense need, her fingers clawing at my shirt, ripping the buttons off as she yanked the fabric apart to reveal my skin. She sat up, lost her jacket, and then pulled her long-sleeved shirt over her head before falling onto me once more.

I wrapped my palm around her nape, devouring her mouth with mine, dominating her with my tongue. She groaned, her nails biting into my shoulder.

It all fucking hurt.

She'd shredded me.

Beat me.

Nearly slayed my heart.

Yet I couldn't say no to this woman, my blood loss doing nothing to stop my raging hard-on. I wanted her. I *needed* her. She must have felt the same, her touch moving south to yank down my zipper and unbutton my pants. Then she shifted to remove her own jeans, the holster for the bullets going with it.

My vision blackened as I tried to move, my side refusing to let me help.

By the time I came back to, she was completely naked and straddling me again, her soaking pussy against my throbbing shaft.

"Fuck," I bit out, hoarse and bruised and broken for her.

She shifted, finding the right angle to lift and sink down on my aching cock. I growled low in my throat, my body in exquisite agony as my immortality began to heal me while her slick cunt forced pleasure to zip straight to my damn balls.

It was a feral mating.

A battle between two warriors destined to kill the other.

And it was hot as fuck.

So damn sinful, so severe, so *us*.

Her tits met my chest as her mouth took mine, our hips pumping into each other, driving us toward the euphoric anguish we both craved.

I wanted to roll her under me, pound her into the cement below, but my body refused to do anything other than accept her punishment. It hurt in the best way. I could hardly breathe, at points I couldn't even see, yet I felt each excruciating second of blissful intoxication.

I was addicted to her.

Just as I'd always been.

I loved her.

Yearned for her.

Would never be the same without her.

She wanted an apology, but all I had to give her was my heart. Truly. As I'd demonstrated by allowing her to nearly pierce it with her stake.

"I hate you," she cried out, her mouth a prayer against mine. "I love you. I'm sorry. Fuck, Cassius. I'm *sorry*."

"Don't apologize." I thrust up into her. "Fuck me, slayer. Live in the moment. Take me into the future." It came out hoarse and wrong, but the flash in her gaze told me she understood every word.

She pressed her palm to my chest, right above my heart, feeling the wound she'd created, and fucked me harder.

Our relationship wasn't normal.

We embraced our inner animals. Because fuck normal. It bored us both. We needed this to thrive.

Her sweet heat clamped around me as a heartfelt moan parted her lips, her orgasm an invitation to dance in another realm of existence. I allowed her to pull me with her, my dick throbbing and pulsating inside her, claiming my slayer in the most depraved of ways.

She was filled with my seed.

My pleasure.

My very essence.

I released my mouth from hers, going to her neck, and bit down on the vein I craved. She screamed, another climax taking her under as I fed on her life, replenishing my own.

We were bonded in a manner no one else could ever understand. Vampires might not take mates, but I declared this female as mine. My soul married hers. My heart belonged to her. There would never be another, just as there had never been anyone else.

She'd possessed me from that very first moment.

My dark enchantment.

My little killer.

My Kseniya.

Wherever she went, I would follow. Even if that meant returning to her former realm. We were in this together now. For eternity.

"I love you," I whispered, darkness threatening to take me as my body demanded time to heal.

"I love you, too," she replied, lying on top of me. "Thank you, Cassius."

My lips curled. "You're welcome, Kseniya." *For everything. For always. For us.*

## EPILOGUE

*A Week Later*

JUDE SAT BEHIND HIS DESK, his dark eyes giving nothing away. "So you're leaving E.V.I.E."

"I don't really have a choice." After everything Grigori had done, I needed to return to my home realm. "But I can wrap up the last case before I go."

He snorted. "You mean the hybrid? Alaric's already taken care of it."

I blinked. "What?"

"You were gone a week, Violet. What did you expect him to do? Wait for you to get back?"

I pinched my lips to the side. It wasn't like I'd meant to disappear for that long. Things had just gotten a little carried away in my home realm. "My priorities..."

"Have shifted," he finished for me. "Yes, I know. Have you spoken to Rowan about it?"

"Not yet," I admitted. "I tried to call her when I got back"—after I'd purchased a replacement phone since the vampires at the club had kept mine as a souvenir—"but she didn't answer. She's my next stop."

He nodded. "I imagine she has some things to tell you as well."

"Yeah? Like what?"

He shrugged. "It's her story to tell, not mine."

Always so vague while implying that he knew things he shouldn't at the same time. "I'm going to miss your cryptic ways."

"No, you're not. You'll be too busy slaying."

I smiled. "True." I had a stake with Grigori's name on it. Of course, we needed to find Anastasia first. Sapphire kept saying we were close—that was what had kept me in my home realm for a week.

After seven days of hearing the same thing from her mouth, Cassius had helped me pop back to the E.V.I.E. universe to check in with Rowan. Then I'd realized that Jude had to be wondering what the hell had happened to me. So I'd ventured here, which had turned into me giving my notice.

I couldn't juggle both. Not right now. Maybe I'd return again in the future after I sorted things out with the Vampire Dynasty, but I suspected that wouldn't be anytime soon.

"Any idea where Alaric is? I'd like to apologize to him."

"He's already off on another mission," Jude replied. "But I'll let him know." He started pulling open drawers, searching for something. "Before you go," he started, bending to pull out a small box from his desk. "Take this."

"What is it?" I asked.

"Open it." He pushed it across the wood and gave me an expectant look.

"Okay." I lifted the lid and found a watch inside. My brow furrowed as I pulled it out to examine the frozen clock face. "Uh, Jude?" I set the empty box back on his desk and held the watch up with an expression that said, *What the hell am I supposed to do with this?*

"Do me a favor and keep that nearby. An alert will sound if I need you."

*Uh, what?* "An alert?"

"Yep." He didn't elaborate, just smiled. "If it goes off, I expect you to get your ass back here because it means I really need you."

"Um, maybe my resignation wasn't clear," I said. "But—"

"Once a slayer, always a slayer," he cut in. "There's no such thing as resigning, Violet. You know that." He gave me an indulgent look, then pushed away from his desk to walk over to his prized companion. "Also, Hades will expect visits from his Luci. So be sure to send her back once you figure out the amulet thing."

"My amulet doesn't work like that."

He merely smiled. "Talk to Rowan. I think she has a few things to tell you."

Yeah, now I was even more intrigued. "Okay. I'll do that."

"Good. See you soon, V." He winked at me, then went to his haunches to pet Hades. "And you'll see Luci soon, too."

I left his office with the watch in one hand and my phone in the other, but my call to Rowan went straight to voicemail. I pocketed the mobile, then slid the watch over my wrist and found the fit oddly perfect.

Cassius stood waiting outside in an all-black suit, his phone to his ear as he dealt with his own life in this realm. He had a few properties and a company to sell. Or give away. He hadn't decided yet. Not to mention his ridiculous King Kaos reputation among the vampires. I suspected he intended to keep that moniker.

When he hung up, I said, "I think we're going to be trapped between two worlds for a bit."

"Yeah?" He wrapped his arm around me as we started walking. "Why do you say that?"

"Because I have unfinished business with Rowan, and I really owe Alaric an apology."

Cassius snorted. "Rowan, yes. Alaric, no. He knew there was a hybrid problem and dragged you into it. If anyone owes someone an apology, it's him."

I stopped walking to face him. "You mentioned a war before, too," I hedged. "What all do you know?"

"That the wolves are having a bit of a turf war with the vampires in this city, and Alaric is at the heart of it," he replied without missing a beat.

"Are you saying he caused it?"

"No, I'm saying he's trying to fix it. But from what I understand, it wasn't his mess; he's just inherited it as the new alpha." He shrugged. "Leadership has its perks. Dealing with shit like this is not one of them." He glanced down at the sidewalk, then back at me. "Am I allowed to walk again, or is there more to discuss?"

"You could have told me all that from the beginning," I muttered. "Instead of sending me on a fool's errand."

"I believe you have Alaric to thank for that more than me, little killer. He's the one who didn't reveal his secrets."

Yeah, that was fair. It also made me feel a little better about leaving him to handle the hybrid mess.

"Rowan's phone keeps going to voicemail," I said, resuming our walk as a way of confirming he was off the hook for more answers. For now. "I don't want to go back until I talk to her. I should probably call Emerald, too."

"Sounds like a boring task list," Cassius drawled.

"Then I guess you'll have to find a way to entertain yourself while I work," I shot back.

His lips curled into a taunting grin. "Oh, that sounds like a challenge."

"Isn't that the story of our lives?" I asked him. "A constant battle of wills and mysteries to solve?"

"I can't imagine a better existence," he admitted softly,

pulling me into his side. "You'll always be my favorite challenge."

I smiled. That was almost sweet, and oddly, it summarized exactly how I felt.

Cassius was my biggest pain in the ass and the best conquest of my life.

We'd survived with all the odds stacked against us, and we'd continue to fight those odds with every breath. Together. Side by side. In this destiny neither of us had chosen, yet found ourselves walking toward nonetheless.

I linked my fingers with his, making him a promise without words. *To have and to hold... till death do us part.*

## The end for now.

Curious to learn more about the real Romanov bloodline? Check out the Vampire Dynasty series by Elle Christensen & Lexi C. Foss. This isn't a fairy tale. It's dark, violent, and underlined in brutal betrayal. Stake up. It's going to be a bloody affair.

Want to know what happens with Alaric? Find out in Crossed Fates, a Kingdom of Wolves story.

Or consider visiting the future with Sapphire in Sapphire Slays.

Craving more vampires? Check out the Blood Alliance series. Just be warned, these heroes are unapologetically alpha, harsh, and don't hold back in the bedroom (or outside of it). #GetBitten

## CROSSED FATES
## A KINGDOM OF WOLVES NOVEL

*Welcome to the Kingdom of Wolves.*
*Careful. These alphas bite.*

### Alaric

Here's the thing about alphas—we don't submit. It's how I ended up as a lone wolf without a pack. I refused to challenge my older brother for the alpha throne, and now I slay monsters for a living.

So the hot little redhead I just saved on my latest mission? Yeah, I have no problem taming her. Except my wolf thinks she's my fated mate.

No, thanks. I'm good.
Only, fate has other plans for us both.

My older brother's just been poisoned, so I'm headed back to a family I no longer know. And the gorgeous female my wolf wants to claim is in the driver's seat beside me. Why? Because she f*cking stabbed me.

Fated mates? Yeah, more like fated hate.

### Makayla

One day, you're hunting a jackhole hybrid with a penchant for abducting women. And the next, you're staring into the eyes of your future mate.

At least that's what this alpha wolf seems to think.

He's tempting, sure. But I'm not interested in anything long-term.

Sometimes, love can be worth the risk.
And sometimes, it'll kill you.
Let the mating games begin.

**Authors' Note:** *Crossed Fates* is a standalone shifter romance with dark undertones. Alaric is all possessive alpha wolf, and Makayla is all fiery stubborn female. Together, they're explosive and passionate. There will be heat. There will be death. There will be biting. Enjoy.

Available on Amazon

## FIRST KISS OF REVENGE
## VAMPIRE DYNASTY, BOOK ONE

*Three dynasties.*
*Two monarchs.*
*One war.*

### Nikola Romanov
My destiny is paved in blood.

Slayer. Slave. Vampire. Pawn.

All titles apply after a dethroned vampire king turns me into a well-trained pet. Now he wants me to take down the renowned assassin guarding the Vampire Dynasty throne. In exchange for my cooperation, I'll be given my freedom.

All right, Master. I'll dance. And when I'm done, I'll burn the entire f*cking dynasty to the ground.

It's the Romanov slayer legacy, after all.

### Dimitri Ivanov

Grigori Rasputin thinks he's bested me. He's wrong. I've added a new player to the board, and she's going to paint his world in red.

Nikola is mine to train.
She's a weapon.
Maybe even my lover.
Whatever I choose.

By the time we're through, Grigori's entire empire will crumble to the ground. Then I'll pick up the pieces of my former throne.

The Vampire Dynasty will thrive again because nothing will stand in my way of taking back what's mine. Not even *her*.

Be a good pet and do as you're told, Nikola darling. I promise this will all be over soon.

**Authors' Note:** This is a dark paranormal romance trilogy featuring overarching themes that will be resolved over the three books. Each couple has a happily-for-now ending in their respective book, with strings that tie the entire trilogy together in the end.

**FIND ON AMAZON**

SAPPHIRE SLAYS

Oops! Sapphire seems to have stolen her blurb. She'll return it at some point. Probably when her wolfish mate forces her hand. Or is he a vampire? Only the future knows…

*USA Today* Bestselling Author Lexi C. Foss loves to play in dark worlds, especially the ones that bite. She lives in Atlanta, Georgia with her husband and their furry children. When not writing, she's busy crossing items off her travel bucket list, or chasing eclipses around the globe. She's quirky, consumes way too much coffee, and loves to swim.

Want access to the most up-to-date information for all of Lexi's books? Sign-up for her newsletter here.

Lexi also likes to hang out with readers on Facebook in her exclusive readers group - Join Here.

*Where To Find Lexi:*
www.LexiCFoss.com

Happily Ever Bitten

## X-Clan Series - Dystopian Paranormal

Andorra Sector

X-Clan: The Experiment

Winter's Arrow

Bariloche Sector

## Vampire Dynasty - Dark Paranormal

Violet Slays

Sapphire Slays

Crossed Fates

First Bite of Revenge

## Other Books

Scarlet Mark - Standalone Romantic Suspense